WINTER GOLD

Recovering from a bereavement, Katie Robertson finds an advertisement for a temporary job on the Isles of Scilly that involves looking after a housebound elderly lady for a few weeks. Hoping to investigate a possible family connection, she eagerly applies. But the woman's grandson, Rory, objects to her presence and believes she's involved with sabotaging the family flower farm. With an unlikely attraction growing between them, can Katie's suspicion of the real culprit be proved correct, and lead to happiness?

Books by Sheila Spencer-Smith
in the Linford Romance Library:

SHEILA SPENCER-SMITH

WINTER GOLD

Complete and Unabridged

LINFORD
Leicester

First published in Great Britain in 2018

First Linford Edition
published 2019

A catalogue record for this book is available
from the British Library.

ISBN 978–1–4448–4036–0

Published by
F. A. Thorpe (Publishing)
Anstey, Leicestershire

Set by Words & Graphics Ltd.
Anstey, Leicestershire
Printed and bound in Great Britain by
T. J. International Ltd., Padstow, Cornwall

This book is printed on acid-free paper

1

Nothing Ventured . . .

Katie Robertson gazed at the job advertisement on her computer screen.

'The question is, Anna, do you think I look suitably mature?'

Her friend laughed.

'Why d'you ask?'

'An older person is needed, it seems.' Katie's hands flew to her head. 'I'll dye my hair grey and wear long skirts and baggy tops. Flat shoes, of course. Lace-ups.'

'That won't do it. The interviewer — what's his name, Rory Hobson, will see through you in seconds.'

Katie held out her leg to look critically at her elegant sandal.

' 'Informal chat' was what he said on the phone.'

Anna was slow in answering this time

because she pretended to consider. Then she spoke, trying not to laugh.

'He won't believe his luck.'

'I'm serious, Anna,' Katie said with feeling. 'I want this job.'

And so she did — and would do anything to get it. Well, almost anything.

Anna read the words on the screen that Katie knew as well as if she had written them herself.

Are you a suitably mature person happy in her own company and fond of walking?

We are looking for someone who is willing to look after a housebound lady on the Isles of Scilly for up to four weeks while her future is being decided. You would be required to do a little housework, prepare and cook light meals and the necessary shopping.

A first-aid qualification is essential. The cottage on St Mary's is isolated in an area of outstanding natural beauty with coastal views of the off-islands.'

'Sounds a lonely life to me,' she

mused. 'Where did you find it?'

'On Working Quest's website. It's for people wanting to travel. You just have to do a few hours of light housework a day in exchange for board and lodging.'

'And you're happy with that?'

Katie's shoulders stiffened. Then suddenly, she relaxed, and turned to look at her friend. She couldn't help laughing.

'I sound a bit mad, don't I?'

'And you really have no idea what this Rory Hobson is like?'

'Not until I meet him. And don't look at me like that! Come on, Anna, it's the job I want — not the man. It's more than likely he's ancient himself — probably the brother of this lady he's so keen to fix up.'

'Of course he isn't. He's someone who cares, that's all. He'll be tall and dark with deep passionate eyes.' Anna gazed into space, a smile on her lips.

Katie giggled.

For a moment Anna was silent. Then her voice lightened.

'Ah, well, you know best. Make the most of your opportunities, girl. That's what I say. This could be your last chance.'

'Thanks.'

Still smiling, Katie turned her chair to face Anna. She smelled her friend's perfume, a light flowery scent that suited her gentle personality. She wondered about her own, less subtle one. Maybe she should start wearing something an elderly lady would appreciate . . . lavender water, perhaps, or eau de cologne?

'Joking apart, I'd like to give it a go.' She had a sudden vision of her father's loving face. He would have been the first to approve and wish her luck. He would have understood as well why she wanted this particular job.

Anna gave Katie a swift hug.

'Take no notice of me,' she said. 'I'm anxious about you, that's all. This Rory Hobson's made it plain he doesn't want someone straight from school, that's all. Of course you'll get the job.'

'You think so?'

'I know so. I'm pleased for you, Katie. You deserve a break. Go for it, girl.' And then, spoiling her encouraging words, she added, 'For whatever reason.'

★   ★   ★

'So, tell me exactly why you think you want this position.'

Katie gazed at the man leaning back in his chair on the other side of the café table. He seemed supremely sure of himself in his deep blue shirt and light jeans.

'Think?' she countered. 'I've been doing a lot more than thinking, Mr Hobson.'

'Rory, please. More coffee?'

She passed her cup to him. From the moment she had entered the café and made herself known to this tall, good-looking man, his expression had changed from polite interest to one she could only describe as disapproving.

Surely there was nothing wrong with the way she looked? His casual wear was not so different from her own. Apart from the dangling earrings, of course, which probably wouldn't have suited him.

He might think her choice of jewellery was too frivolous for one keen to take on what sounded like a responsible position, for all the lightness in the wording of his advertisement.

Sunshine slanted in through the high window, highlighting the table arrangement of scented narcissi in front of her. They seemed to promise a spring day outside instead of one where blustery autumn leaves were blowing about in the chilly wind. The bright flowers seemed as inappropriate as her meeting with this man who at first sight she might have thought pleasing with his wavy hair and blue eyes.

He poured more coffee.

'I thought I'd made it plain that a mature person was needed,' he said now in his deep voice. Definitely a capable man quick to make judgements.

She inclined her head as she accepted her cup. She could make swift judgments, too, especially about people who doubted her suitability for a position for which she knew she was experienced.

He leaned forward.

'But tell me about yourself.'

This was better. She took a deep breath.

'I worked with a firm of solicitors in Exeter for several years after I left college, secretarial work. Then I looked after my father here in Truro for nearly three more. I did some part-time work in a craft shop for a while until I needed to be a full-time carer. I did a first-aid course at a local college. I have a certificate to prove it.'

She reached for her bag beneath her seat, but paused on seeing his swift dismissive gesture.

'That won't be necessary. You included a copy with your application.' His voice

7

was expressionless.

'I thought this job was exactly what I was looking for,' she said, her voice firm.

'It's a lonely life. Jarrel Cottage is isolated. The nearest shop is two miles away and there's virtually no transport in the winter months. You need inner resources to be able to cope with that.'

'But in an area of outstanding natural beauty.'

'Natural beauty isn't everything, outstanding or not.'

Anna would love that remark, Katie thought. Was he implying that she had inner beauty as well as the landscape? She rather thought not. She bit back a smile.

'You're aware of what your duties would be?'

'That's why I'm here.'

'And you know it might only be for a maximum of four weeks?'

She nodded.

'There is someone interested in purchasing my father's flat,' she said,

8

just in case he was in any doubt that she would pull out of the agreement. 'I need somewhere else temporary to live while I decide what to do next. This seemed an ideal situation. Perfect, in fact.'

He gave her a swift questioning look.

'Only for someone of mature years,' he said. He drained the last of his coffee and put the cup down with a determined clunk. 'As I said, I'm looking for someone who is able to handle a person I have to admit is rather difficult. May I ask your age?'

She felt odd sitting here discussing something that, since she had turned thirty, was a sensitive subject. She was pleased to see his surprised expression when she told him.

He cleared his throat.

'I see. Your references are in good order but I don't think . . . '

She finished her own coffee and stood up.

'I'm beginning to think that I'm wasting my time here, Mr Hobson.'

'Wait! I haven't finished. You don't understand. My grandmother is a stubborn woman. She's refusing to move and she's highly suspicious of anyone being forced on her. She might well refuse you entry.'

She looked at him through narrowed eyes.

'Grandmother?'

'You think I look too old to have one of those?'

She thought she caught a flicker of amusement but couldn't be sure.

'So she has the same name as yourself — Hobson?'

'Not too amazing, is it? Hannah Jane Hobson, my father's mother.'

This definitely put a different slant on things. Hannah Jane Hobson. Too much of a coincidence, surely?

'Please sit down again, Miss, er, Robertson. I still can't imagine why you should want this job.'

She wanted it even more now. Hannah Jane Hobson! This couldn't have been better. She hadn't told Anna the main reason why this job sounded like fate. In fact she hadn't told anybody.

She stared him straight in the eyes.

'May I ask if you've had many applicants?'

His answer was in his slight hesitation. The obstinate grandmother, of course, she thought, dismissing that immediately. This job was meant for her. He'd been upfront about that and she admired his honesty.

'It's early days yet,' he said.

She straightened her shoulders.

'You obviously need someone at once. And that someone is going to be me.'

He stood up, towering above her in a way that could have been intimidating.

'You seem very sure.'

'Please check my references again.'

A beat of silence and then a flicker of a smile.

'Very well. Expect to hear from me in a day or two.'

'Thank you.'

Before he had time to object, she

moved swiftly to the door. Rory Hobson had just got himself the right person to look after his obstinate relation, she thought, even if he didn't appreciate it yet.

2

Unexpected Arrival

It was a wonder the taxi driver knew Jarrel Cottage, situated as it was some way from the small and only town on the largest of the five inhabited islands of the Isles of Scilly.

'Are you here for long?' he asked as he manoeuvred his vehicle along the quay and then drove slowly through the narrow streets.

Katie smiled.

'A few weeks, I expect. I've come here to work, to look after an old lady.'

'Mrs Hobson?'

'That's the one.'

This was something she was going have to get used to. Everybody knowing who everybody was. A small island, after all.

'She's expecting you?' he asked.

From the surprise in his voice Mrs Hobson's reputation of being fiercely independent was well known. He must be thinking she was taking a risk in coming here at all, Katie thought.

'She's a fine woman,' he added. 'You'll do well if she takes to you. As one of her former pupils I can vouch for that.'

'She was a schoolteacher?'

'One of the old school. You didn't dare put a foot wrong.' He laughed.

Katie was silent. So Mrs Hobson was bossy as well as stubborn? Well, good. She respected people with spirit.

'I'm hoping Mrs Hobson is expecting me today,' she said. She had phoned Jarrel Cottage but got no answer. Because time was pressing she had then tried Jarrel Farm itself and left a message with someone who sounded young and enthusiastic. Time would tell what happened next.

Now there were tantalising views of the harbour and glimpses of sandy beaches before they passed small fields bounded by high hedges of a shrub she didn't recognise.

'Pittosporum,' the driver told her when she asked. 'Excellent for shelter for the bulb fields. It's needed, too, in some of the winter storms when the winds sweep in from the Atlantic.'

Katie shivered in anticipation although it was hard to imagine on this balmy November day.

They were bumping down a track now and the potholes, full of water, glinted in the sunshine. She saw a cottage near the top of a slope with blue sky and fluffy clouds behind it. With the sunshine full on the front it looked solid and dependable.

There were small windows on either side of the protruding porch and two more upstairs, and a slate roof with a chimney pot on one edge of it.

'This is it.'

The driver drew the car to a halt and they got out. Soon her suitcase and travel bag were on the ground but before the driver could lift them up again, Katie put out a restraining hand.

'I'm all right, really,' she said. 'I can manage.'

'You're sure?'

She heaved them up and watched the driver reverse his vehicle to return the way he had come. Then she unlatched the gate and walked up the short path to the door. She took an enormous breath and rang the doorbell.

Without warning, she was overcome by a sense of loneliness. What was she doing here amongst strangers, far from home without her father's loving presence? But three long months had passed since Dad died.

She swallowed a lump in her throat and wondered why it was making her so emotional at this moment. At home she had coped, throwing herself into packing up the house, deciding what should go into store, cleaning the place. Tears were rolling down her cheeks and she had no spare hand to wipe them away because she was gripping her luggage as if she was afraid that it, too, would desert her.

There was the sound of footsteps and the door opened. Katie straightened and tried to swallow back her tears.

'Can I help you?' The formal high-necked blouse had a cameo at the neck and the black skirt was long. For a moment Katie thought she had gone back in time.

'Oh, um . . . ' She gulped. 'Sorry . . . did you get my phone message about arriving today? I'm Katie. Katie Robertson. I spoke to someone at Jarrel Farm.'

'My grandson, Mark, undoubtedly.'

'He sounded young.'

There was a moment of hesitation before the woman spoke again.

'Come in. It looks as if you've come to stay.' There was a long appraising look from shrewd grey eyes.

'I'd very much like to.'

'I can't help you with your luggage. Put it down over there.'

Katie did as she was told, feeling for

a tissue to wipe her face.

'Come through to the kitchen.'

After the brightness outside, the small hall was dark but now Katie saw that the walls were covered in some sort of woven material in a deep maroon unrelieved by any picture or photograph.

A door at the further end opened into the kitchen, which smelled slightly of mint. In here a bright dresser stood against one yellow wall crammed with blue and white china. The effect was eye-catching.

'Mrs Hobson?' Katie said. 'I . . . '

'Yes, that's me. Jane. And you? You're looking perplexed.'

'It's Mrs Hannah Hobson I expected to see.'

'And that's exactly who I am, Hannah Jane Hobson.'

'You weren't expecting me today?'

'Never mind that. First things first. Sit down.'

Katie pulled out a chair from the table and saw a bright tapestry-covered cushion on it.

'Oh, that's lovely.'

'My own work,' Jane Hobson said, as if she hated to admit it.

She opened the lid on one of the hot plates on the Aga and pushed a kettle on to it. Then she placed a single cup and saucer nearby. Pausing for a moment, she took a deep breath and reached up for another from the dresser.

Katie leaped up.

'Here, let me.'

Mrs Hobson's face paled.

'Please sit down,' she said, her voice sharp. 'I shall make tea and we shall have it here.'

Reluctantly Katie obeyed. From the smart way the older woman was dressed she obviously cared a lot about how others viewed her, and her weakness now in front of a stranger must be galling. Katie understood this completely.

She clenched her hands together and tried hard to concentrate on the ticking clock on the dresser and the way the hand hardly seemed to move.

Her wish to help was natural but stupid in the circumstances. Dad had let her do a lot for him but she suspected it was for her good and not his.

Katie accepted the cup and saucer offered and placed them carefully in front of her. The steam rose in the quiet air. The silence between them was painful.

'Your grandson wanted me to come to be with you for a while to be of help,' Katie said at last.

'So Mark's up to his tricks again, is he? I might have known it.'

'We're talking at cross purposes. I haven't met him yet. It was Rory I saw at the interview.'

Jane looked startled.

'Interview?'

'You didn't know anything about that?'

'I know nothing about any interview.'

'Rory Hobson wanted to meet me before I came, you see. We had coffee together in Truro.'

'So you're a friend of his?'

'Well, no.' Not yet, Katie was going to say but then thought better of it. No-one could assume friendship between them, not even Anna back there in Truro letting her imagination run away with her.

'Rory needed to know what I was like before he offered me the job,' she said.

'Job?' Jane Hobson's voice was icy. 'I wish I could understand what's going on. Mark's been trying to hustle me out of here for weeks but I'm having none of it.'

Katie picked up her cup and took a careful sip before putting it down again. There were yellow daffodils painted on the outside with butterflies hovering around them. Would butterflies be around at the same time as daffodils?

She hardly thought so. Probably as unlikely as her being welcome here. But how was any of it her fault? She had come a long way to help out where help was needed.

21

'I still don't understand. You're not some sort of social worker?'

'I don't think a social worker would turn up on your doorstep with her luggage, do you?' Katie said with spirit.

'Perhaps not.' Jane stirred a teaspoon of sugar into her tea and put the spoon down.

Katie looked at Rory Hobson's indomitable grandmother. It sounded very much as if he and Mark had got together on this. If Mark wanted his grandmother out of this cottage, then what about Rory? For some reason that hurt in a way she couldn't explain.

'And so Rory insisted on someone moving in with me?'

Katie nodded.

'Just for a week or two.'

The silence again was profound but in it Katie thought she saw a glimmer of hope.

'I recognise unhappiness when I see it,' Jane Hobson said, as if the words were dragged out of her, 'and I've a feeling there's more here than meets the eye. Very well. I shall let you unpack now.'

'Thank you.'

'The back bedroom will suit you, I think, but the bed isn't made. And be careful of the stairs. They're rather awkward to negotiate, I'm afraid, but I shall come up with you and find everything that's needed.'

Her sudden kindness was over-whelming.

3

Time to Explore

The bedroom, with its own bathroom, was small but charming, made so, Katie thought, by the beautiful patchwork quilt on the bed. Some of the colours were picked up in the curtains and in the pale blue of the walls. She liked the white furniture, too, and the fresh look it gave was appealing.

She ran her hands over the lovely colours of the quilt.

'Did you make this, too? It's beautiful.'

Jane Hobson looked pleased.

'There are several more. I bring them out sometimes for an airing. People don't seem to want them nowadays.'

Her voice was matter of fact but a small sigh escaped her as she straightened a corner of the quilt that didn't need straightening. Katie took it from her as she started to remove it.

'Please, let me.'

Jane relinquished it and Katie folded it carefully to place it on the chest beneath the window while she made the bed with the sheets and blankets her hostess took out of the airing cupboard on the landing.

The pillowcases were on a higher shelf, and Jane needed Katie to reach them.

'I had a small operation on my shoulder a week or two ago,' Jane said in explanation. 'I have to be a little careful, you see.' She smiled. 'Silly, isn't it?'

'Far from silly, especially as I'm here to help you.'

'I knew I was allergic to plaster, the ordinary kind, but then it turned out I'm allergic to any kind of plaster as well, so I can't have a suitable dressing on it and there's a risk of infection.'

Katie was aware that she mustn't

show her sympathy or Jane might be offended.

'They're looking after it, aren't they?' she said. 'I mean, someone has a look at it for you?'

'Glenda, our community nurse, is very good. Yes, I'm well looked after. But now Rory seems to think I need more care, does he? He must think I'm a feeble old woman and I don't like that. How long does he expect you to stay?'

Katie hesitated. This was an awkward question. Jane seemed too good a person to deserve anything less than the truth.

'I think the best thing is to show you a copy of the advertisement I answered,' she said, 'and then you can see for yourself. Let me put this lovely quilt back on again and then I'll show you.'

Jane sat down and looked at her expectantly.

Katie had printed the piece out from the website and stuffed it in her bag just before leaving home. She found it quickly and handed it over. It wasn't easy watching Jane reading the words, frowning a little in concentration and looking unhappier by the minute.

'Your accommodation is on the first floor of the cottage,' Jane read aloud after she had perused the first part, 'with an en suite bathroom. Afternoons will be free. You will also have the opportunity to earn money working as a picker in the bulb fields if desired.'

She looked at Katie in silence for a moment before handing the paper back to her.

'Thank you for showing me.' She laughed a little uncertainly as she got to her feet. 'Rory seems to be insisting on someone much older. So how is it that you're here instead, Katie?'

'I rather forced it on him, I'm afraid.'

'Then you're a clever girl. No-one ever forces Rory's hand when he's made up his mind to what he believes is right.' The twinkle in Jane's eyes vanished. 'So now I know where I stand. Rory thinks a decision about my future is needed. It sounds ominous. I

27

could have believed it of Mark but not of Rory. I shall go downstairs and think about this while you get settled in.'

'So you're not going to throw me out?'

'You're a good girl, Katie. Mature person indeed, the very idea! I'd have had none of that if he'd seen fit to consult me.'

Katie waited until Jane had gone downstairs one step at a time, leaning carefully on the banisters and breathing heavily as if they were almost too much for her. Then she started her unpacking.

At the bottom of her suitcase she had packed an old sampler and now she lifted it out and spread it on the bed, remembering how she had found it in the bottom drawer of Dad's bureau when sorting through his belongings a few days after the funeral. Intrigued, she had examined it carefully and then folded it into its tissue paper to keep safely with the rest of her things as a treasured possession.

Out of the depths of memory came

something Mum's aunt had said about the group of islands out in the Atlantic, where narcissi grew that were harvested in winter time and sent up to London for folk to buy. The daffodils round the edge of the sampler had seemed significant as soon as she saw the advertisement placed online by someone with the same family name.

'Hannah Amy Hobson's work in the year 1860,' she read aloud from the sampler.

The words in dark green looked as if they had been worked painstakingly, probably the last stitches done by a young girl of what . . . ten, eleven? The patience of it!

She marvelled at the perfect stitches all combining to make a beautiful picture of a garden scene. Never in a million years could she contemplate doing such work.

Now, looking down at it on her bed, she knew she must show it to Jane. But for the moment she placed it in the spare drawer in her bedside table.

For the first time since her dad died, she felt a rush of adrenalin that was life-empowering. She hoped it would last for the weeks that she was needed here. If needed she was.

★ ★ ★

Downstairs again Katie found Jane seated at the kitchen table waiting for her. Jane closed the magazine she was reading and removed her glasses.

'I shall go into the sitting-room for my afternoon nap now,' she said. 'And you, Katie, shall have some time off as the advertisement said. We must stick to the rules.'

If she hadn't looked so serious Katie would have suspected she were joking.

Jane struggled to her feet.

'This is a good time, I think,' she said, 'for you to take a look outside and explore the immediate surroundings.'

'If you're sure?'

'Go along now.'

'I won't be long, then, just a quick

walk to get my bearings.'

Katie put on her walking boots and with her jacket zipped up she headed to the top of the track that had looked so intriguing when she arrived. She found it turned a sharp right to lead down to the coastal path with the glittering blue of the sea beyond. The tufts of grass growing on it proved it was less used here and there were no potholes. Instead there were jewel-like glints of tiny particles in the rocky surface.

To the left were grass-covered stone walls bordering small fields and rising ground culminated in a headland with fir trees on the top. And of course, ahead of her was the awe-inspiring sea dotted with islands.

She paused to take it all in. The feeling of space was incredible. The breeze stirred her hair and she smiled, thinking how lucky she was to be here.

She paused to watch the thin line of white surging against the rocky shores of the nearest smaller islands, some of them hardly more than areas of rock.

There were tiny houses on the larger one out there in the distance and some lovely beaches.

Her fingers itched for the camera she had left on the chest of drawers in her bedroom. She would spend longer here another day with time to look around and explore further.

But now she must get back. She needed to familiarise herself with the daily running of Jarrel Cottage so she could suggest ways where she might be useful. She would need all her tact and sensitivity for the task ahead. Determination, too.

She went to the back door of the cottage and into the kitchen to change into her indoor shoes. She hung her jacket on the hook near the door and went into the hall.

The sound of voices in the sitting room made her pause. She heard Jane's soft tones and a male voice that sounded deep and authoritative.

'Open the door, Rory,' she heard Jane say. 'I think I heard someone coming in

the back way. I think Katie's here now.'
  The door opened.

4

Handsome – But Maddening!

Katie's smile wasn't as confident as she would have wished when she went in to the sitting-room. To make up for it she squared her shoulders and looked directly at Rory.

In his thick sweater and jeans, he seemed larger than she remembered and surprisingly attractive. She took a deep breath and reminded herself that this was the man who had scorned her at the interview and she mustn't forget it.

Jane, seated on the sofa in front of the window, smiled at Katie with kindness.

'You've met my grandson, of course, Katie?'

'A day or two ago,' Rory answered for her, moving back a little so that his presence wasn't so threatening in the small, overcrowded room.

'So you admit placing the advertisement in that underhand way, Rory?' Jane said, looking at him with that direct gaze Katie was beginning to know well.

He smiled slightly.

'You know I have your best interests at heart? That's why I'm here now.'

'I'm pleased you had the sense to send Katie to me, but I'm not sure I like the way you set about it. And I'm certainly not about to replace her with this woman you mention.' Her tone was harsher than her usual soft one.

'Another applicant and far more suitable, as I told you.' He spoke with force. 'I felt duty bound to tell you.'

Jane snorted.

'Duty!'

In front of Jane was a low table painted white holding a pile of magazines and a basket containing an assortment of wool. She pushed it away and stood up.

'Please, sit down, Grandmother,' Rory said. 'You need rest at this time of your life, not confrontation.

'Grandmother?' Jane said with scorn. 'Since when have we been so formal?'

He smiled.

'Gram then, if you prefer.'

'And who said anything about a confrontation?'

Here it came, Katie thought. They had been discussing this before she came in and having it raised again in her presence was embarrassing. She made a movement towards the door but Rory put out a hand to restrain her.

At the same time Jane sat down and patted the seat beside her.

'Come and sit beside me, Katie. This concerns you in a way that Rory won't like. And you sit down too, young man, instead of standing there like some overbearing giant. Or, better still, go and make yourself useful. I think we'd all appreciate a cup of tea.'

'I'll do it,' Katie said.

She was out of the door before Rory

could move but then was disconcerted to find he was following her. She wasn't quite in time to close the kitchen door between them but he did it for her. The trouble was that he was on the wrong side of it and looking at her with his eyebrows raised.

'What?' she said, her voice sharp.

'I can see you've made yourself at home here already.'

His words sounded pleasant enough but there was an undertone of resentment.

'You haven't come to turf me out, have you?' she said with some asperity. 'I don't think you can do that since my contract is for four weeks.'

'My grandmother might have something to say if I tried.'

Katie smiled briefly in acknowledgement.

'We both know she needs looking after,' she said, 'and I'm the right person to do it.'

To prove it, she filled the kettle at the sink, turning the cold tap on as far as it would go with the result that water spurted out over the floor.

He laughed.

She turned her back on him to wipe it up with the floor cloth.

'That was a mistake,' she muttered.

'Like mine the other day.'

This surprised her. She plugged in the kettle and swung round.

'At the interview, you mean?'

'If you like to call it that.'

'I'd call it nothing else.'

He shrugged, a glint in his eyes that was unnerving.

'Just that, then. I was expecting someone in their later years who would be happy in this quiet situation and no longer wanting to get about and do things. Instead there you were looking bright and active and far too elegant.'

Katie frowned. She should have been flattered but he had made assumptions that displeased her. Why should age mean you couldn't do any of the things you loved when you were younger?

Her father had been a keen bird-watcher in his youth and still was in his late seventies. Before he was completely housebound in his last weeks she had often driven him out to some of his favourite places and they enjoyed days out together that had pleased them both. In any case, why wouldn't someone young be happy away from the bustle of life?

Generalisations were horrible.

'So my qualifications counted for nothing?'

He shrugged again.

'Appearances count, I'm afraid.'

Don't they just, she thought. Maybe her facetious suggestions to Anna about what she should wear for the interview weren't so silly after all.

'I should have had more sense than to let you get away with it,' he said. 'I'd like my grandmother to reconsider. This woman sounds excellent: late middle-aged and sensible and knows Scilly well. What would you know of winter here? Conditions can be harsh on the islands.'

She clutched the edge of the table so hard her knuckles showed white.

'I shall appreciate anything Scilly weather throws at me: snow, hail, icy roads . . . '

Again that slight twitch at the sides of his mouth.

'Rain and mud and a lot of it. Atlantic gales sweeping in. Even with higher temperatures than the mainland in the winter, the wind chill factor can make it feel cold.'

'Let me tell you, I'm fully prepared for anything even if you're right about the weather — which I doubt very much.'

'We shall see.'

'What has the weather to do with befriending someone like your grand-mother?'

'We had gales last winter,' he said, 'the aftermath of a hurricane that brought trees down on a neighbouring farm. You might be housebound, too.'

'And?'

'Just think about it.'

She ignored that but continued with the job in hand, struggling not to let him see how objectionable she found him.

Katie set a tray with Jane's blue and white china, milk jug and sugar bowl. The kettle gave a pleasant hum as it came to the boil. She made the tea.

'Biscuits?' he said.

She hesitated.

'In the wall cupboard above you in a tin marked 'Biscuits'. Red with white spots.'

'So you come here often enough to know that?'

She put some chocolate digestives on a plate which she placed on the tray.

'Allow me,' Rory offered as she picked it up.

'I can manage, thank you.'

'Just as you assume you can manage my grandmother and know what's best for her having known her for all of five minutes?'

'I believe she knows what's best for

herself and I shall abide by that. And you must, too. There's no more to be said.'

The china on the tray shook a little as she moved towards the door. He opened it for her, bowing slightly as she passed in front of him.

She then had to wait for him to open the one into the sitting-room.

Jane put down the magazine she was examining and placed her glasses on top of it.

'There's a pattern for a footstool cover in here,' she said. 'I've been looking through my wool and I think I've got enough. Wool embroidery is a new thing for me. It's always good to try something new, don't you think, Katie?'

She cleared a space for the tray.

'Now, let's enjoy our tea and you can tell us, Rory, what's really worrying you.'

5

Forming a Bond

'So you haven't any family of your own, Katie?' Jane Hobson asked later when they were seated at the kitchen table eating the meal of omelettes and salad that Katie had prepared.

Katie had told her that much, but she hadn't mentioned the fact that had been brought home to her when she was invited to Anna's party and she had seen her friend in the midst of her siblings and their families.

Anna hadn't meant her to feel out of it but it hurt all the same. That was not long after the funeral, of course, when she had been at her most vulnerable and Anna would have understood if she had declined the invitation.

Katie had managed to survive the evening — but only just. The next morning she had made a solemn vow that she would pick herself up and do something positive with her life.

She was alone, yes, but she had good friends and the opportunity to go wherever she chose to think things through, a place where she was welcomed by someone who, it seemed, needed her.

Jane finished eating and put down her knife and fork.

'That was very nice. I enjoyed that.'

Katie smiled, pleased to see that her hostess was looking better now. The pink had returned to her cheeks and as she got up from the table she stood upright instead of stooping and clinging to something in support. Katie knew that it was determination and not mere stubbornness that drove her on. She wanted to be in charge of her life and not allow her grandsons to decide what was best for her.

'I didn't ask you, Katie, if you had a good walk earlier?'

'Yes. I couldn't believe how clear

everything was,' Katie said. 'Those islands looked intriguing.'

'The Eastern Isles,' Jane said.

'I could almost see every rock and blade of grass. Are they always like that?'

Jane smiled.

'Rain coming, that's what it means when it's so clear. You'll see how changeable it is here. Sun one moment, rain the next.'

'No time to get bored with one type of weather, then?' Katie glanced at the window, expecting a blackened sky but not seeing it.

Maybe it symbolised how her life would be on Scilly, one moment enjoying the peaceful beauty of the place and the next plunged into controversy in her support of Jane in the face of the logic and determination of her grandsons.

Afterwards she went up to her room and stood for moment looking out of the window. From here she could see the track running down to the coastal path that had looked so intriguing when she walked down for a short way.

She promised herself that one day soon she would go further and see what was round the next bend. A different view of sea and islands, she supposed.

She yawned now and turned away.

Rory had been clever in hiding from his grandmother exactly what he and Mark had in mind for her future. He had spoken briefly of a client of his in Truro who wanted a huge extension built on to her small bungalow on the side of a hill and wasn't going to take no for an answer.

'So, how did you persuade the poor woman to change her mind?' Jane asked.

'With difficulty, I have to say. I should have had Mark with me to use his charm on her, shouldn't I?'

Katie had found it hard not to smile. He was going to find persuading his grandmother to agree to something against her will infinitely harder.

Rory had left soon after that and it

was quiet without his presence.

Katie wouldn't admit it even to herself but the quietness of Jarrel Cottage was a little unnerving.

A diversion was needed and that was why she had come upstairs now.

★   ★   ★

Back in the sitting-room, she spread her precious sampler out on the small table in front of Jane.

'I thought you might like to see this,' she said rather tentatively.

Jane picked up her glasses and leaned forward to examine it.

'What beautiful stitching,' she said, 'and a lovely design.'

She was silent for a moment, deep in thought.

'And the name?' Katie's voice was husky and she cleared her throat.

Jane looked up at her, her eyes slightly misty behind her glasses.

'My husband's aunt had hair the same colour as yours,' she said. 'Her mother kept a lock of it in a locket she always wore. I don't know what happened to it when she died.'

Jane gave a little sigh.

It was a moment charged with emotion. Katie, moving back a little, reminded herself that nothing might come of it.

All the same, she felt strange as if she were in the presence of something stronger than both of them.

'There seems to be a Hannah in every generation of the Hobson family,' Jane said. 'Rory's aunt was Hannah Elizabeth and his great-aunt Hannah Amelia. I always knew her as Aunt Milly. And this little girl who worked the sampler in 1860 was Hannah Amy.'

'Do you think there's a connection?' Katie could hardly speak for the constriction in her throat.

'Undoubtedly.'

The moment was exhilarating.

'This was among my father's possessions when he died,' Katie said. 'I didn't know he had it. My mother's maiden name was Hobson. She died when I was sixteen.'

Jane removed her glasses.

'We need to look out some old photos and see what they tell us.'

'You have photographs of so long ago?'

'Well, no, not as far back as then, of course. But there might be a family likeness. I think I would like to see.'

Her eyes were bright with pleasure and Katie smiled her agreement.

She leaped to help Jane as she got unsteadily to her feet.

'My stick?'

'Here it is.'

The bottom drawer of the bureau was heavy and Katie helped to pull it open. Inside were some ancient-looking tomes.

Jane lifted out the top one and indicated to Katie that she should carry the rest over to the table beside her chair.

'Now, my dear,' she said, once they were seated again. 'Let's see what we have here.'

Her face, normally pale, was flushed and her hands trembled a little as she opened the first page.

'A good place to start is at the beginning,' she said. 'This is the first album of many. There's a good chance we will find something.'

Her confidence was uplifting and it was obvious to Katie that following this tenuous link meant nearly as much to Jane as it did to her.

Excitement rose in her, along with anxiety. One thing was sure, though. Jane would pursue this until something positive emerged.

And this was the reason Katie had come to Scilly.

But looking after Jane's interests was important, too, and it seemed now that they were combined.

★ ★ ★

Rory had rarely been able to fool his grandmother. Even as a small boy she had seen through his weak excuses and explanations. So concerns about his cousin, Mark, and the family flower farm must be erased from his mind or she would get it out of him in no time at all.

He was aware that the family name meant a lot to her and for her to learn that Mark, the only son of her elder son, was letting it slide for whatever reason would break her heart.

Rory glanced at his watch as he drove away from Jarrel Cottage. He had called in at the farm first to tell Mark how things stood with their grandmother, in the hope that they would have a few weeks to come to some arrangement that would suit them all.

He had planned to provide someone as a temporary companion to her, of the same generation with interests in common, but he might just as well not have bothered.

He had little idea of how things would work out now, or even if, one day in the future, Mark might decide enough was enough and move back to the mainland, leaving everything for him to sort out and his grandmother out of a home.

It was the worst scenario, of course, but had to be considered. The future was unsettled and if Rory wasn't careful this worrying about it would affect his own work schedule on the mainland.

Mark had, as usual, only one thing on his mind. The sooner his latest girl-friend realised that he shied away from any sort of commitment the better.

The surprising thing was that when his father died Mark was insistent that, as the only son, he carry on the lease of the farm from the Duchy.

Commitment with a capital C, Rory thought ruefully, but likely to harm the good name of the Hobson family if he made a hash of it.

Standing by and watching him make mistakes was hard for Rory. Some-where along the line Mark had forgotten that he, like Rory, had been brought up to have a respect for his heritage and to have strong ties to family, community and culture.

Plainly Mark was rebelling against it, planning to break with tradition and do something unorthodox. The thought of that was disturbing.

Rory increased speed when he joined the road. Plenty of time to get back to his place, pack his overnight bag and get himself to the airport.

This was a brief visit because of Mark's frantic phone call last evening. Luckily his own work schedule had allowed him to help out in an emergency although he would stick to his original plan and be back on Scilly at the end of the week to spend a few days here anyway.

It was a relief that Mark had got the required number of narcissi to Mainland Marketing on time, but the atmosphere between them had been tense. Mark had shouted something unintelligible and then drove off on business of his own. Trusting to luck was always Mark's philosophy and this time he had done better than he deserved.

Of course, it was abundantly clear that Jarrel Farm needed to diversify if it was to keep its head above water, and Mark had the good sense to see that. Flower farming was a precarious business, relying so much on the weather as it did.

His idea of converting two disused sheds into holiday lets was a good one but he had gone about it in a haphazard way, ending up with two units that were well below the standard looked for in holiday property these days.

Mark had got some unqualified chap in from the mainland to advise, with disastrous results. Rory's own long training as an architect and his successful business in Truro meant nothing to Mark. Rory had disguised his deep hurt at not being consulted as well as he could, but it had been hard.

Arriving in town, Rory stopped to allow a truck to pass in the narrow street and was soon at his cottage overlooking the sea at Porthcressa. Adjoining it were the outhouses he was in the process of renovating, that would mean he could work from home and return to the mainland for a few days a week. He was a well-respected architect now and could afford to create his own client list from personal recommendations.

He smiled as he pulled up, full of confidence again on this lovely day when the islands looked their best. Mark had done well this time in asking for his help. Perhaps he was coming to his senses at last.

Well, good luck to him. Rory hoped he would do well.

6

Words of Warning

Taking care to avoid a large puddle, the community nurse parked her car alongside the wall at the side of Jarrel Cottage. Katie ushered her into the sitting-room where Jane was waiting for her and offered her a cup of tea.

The nurse shook her head.

'First things first, if you don't mind,' she said, smiling in such a friendly way that no-one could possibly take offence. Then she looked at Katie. 'I'm Glenda. I believe my patient is being very well looked after.'

'Looked after?' Jane said, her voice crisp. 'I can perfectly well look after myself. Katie is a very good friend to me, that's all.'

'And we all need one of those,' the nurse said, winking at Katie and at the same time pushing a fair curl of hair back behind her ears from where it immediately bounced out again.

While she was attending to her patient, Katie wandered outside. The scent of newly-mown grass around the cottage hung in the breeze.

The garden looked attractive sur-rounded by the stone walls. The absence of flower-beds was an advan-tage, she thought, because it made you concentrate on the lushness of the grass and notice the occasional glint of mica in the stone.

She could imagine sitting out here on summer afternoons soaking up the sun after having been down for a swim to that attractive little beach she had glimpsed.

In the future Jane might not be living here if her grandsons got their way. Katie thought of Mark's easy confi-dence and Rory's determination. But Jane was strong. She wouldn't give in easily.

A memory of Rory's words of

warning at the interview came back to her and she had a sudden vision of him leaning forward in his chair in the Duchy café, trying to persuade her that she would be unable to cope with such a person.

She smiled, remembering his frown and the way he pushed a lock of hair from a forehead lined with concern, unaware that his warning would have been enough to convince her to come, even if she hadn't had other motives.

Jane had told her to have a good look round the property. That included the building at right angles to the cottage that she had noticed as the taxi drove up only a couple of days ago.

From this angle the cottage looked bigger than she had first thought and solidly comfortable in its setting as if it had been here for generations.

The wide door on the far side of the building creaked as Katie pushed it open and went in. Until her eyes got used to the musty darkness she stood where she was, breathing in the smell of dust and old stone until it occurred to her to prop the door wider open.

The small windows encased in dirt were high up and let in little light. Beneath her feet the earth floor felt as hard as concrete.

In the gloomy depths she saw that stacked against the far wall were several bicycles. She went closer to look. There were five of them, covered in cobwebs and looking as if they had been put there and forgotten years ago.

She pulled one out by its grimy handlebars and sneezed. The machine was old-fashioned and heavy and the basket on the front was full of old cloths. As Katie pulled them out and discarded them something shot out from underneath her feet and skittered across the floor. Startled, she clutched at the bike she was holding or it would have clattered to the floor. A mouse, or worse, a young rat? It was too dusky to see.

She edged the bike away from the others and tried to dust the cobwebs off the saddle. From what she could feel of the tyres they both had a little air left in them. The back brake was hard to pull on but the front one seemed to be functioning.

Great. Old as the bike was, it would get her about. She hadn't ridden one for years, but that was no problem if Jane didn't object. A bit of practice along the local tracks and she'd be fine.

She wheeled the machine to the door and paused outside to rub down her jeans and jersey that had caught some of the filth from her exertions.

Then she pushed the machine across the grass to the cottage just as the community nurse was closing the door behind her.

'You look as if you've been rolling in the dust and dirt,' Glenda said, her mouth turning up at the corners.

Katie grinned.

'How is Mrs Hobson?'

'She'll live. She's more worried about you than she is about herself. She thinks you'll find it too lonely here.'

There was a slight rise in her tone at the end of that, as if she wanted to get something clear, and Katie hastened to reassure her.

'Not a bit of it. It's fine, really. I love the peace and quiet.'

And so she did, she thought. There was a special quality to it that she was beginning to appreciate.

'There's a quiz on down in town tonight. Why don't you come?'

Katie's glance flickered to the bicycle, checking for lights and not seeing any.

'Becky Tait lives fairly close. She'll give you a lift, I'm sure. I'll give her a buzz. What do you say?'

'Well . . . '

'Think about it.'

Grey cloud had covered the sun now and the next second light rain began to fall. The nurse buttoned her coat up to just beneath her chin and pulled up the hood. Then she gave another cheery smile and was gone. Katie, bemused, watched her car bumping over the potholes as if it enjoyed the experience and couldn't get enough of it.

Jane was pleased that Katie had unearthed one of the bicycles that had been in the store for years.

'I left them there when I moved in,' she said. 'They were doing no harm.'

'But why are there five?'

'Well, that I couldn't say. I'll ask Mark next time he comes, whenever that is.'

Jane gave a small sigh as she settled herself on the sofa, trying to find as comfortable a place as she could for her painful shoulder.

The photograph albums were still stacked on the table in front of her and now she opened the second one, ready to continue her search. Since she was happily engrossed, Katie left her to it.

Her duties had been described as light and this morning she enjoyed vacuuming upstairs, though it seemed the bedrooms hardly needed any attention. Both had obviously been recently decorated in different colours and looked fresh and clean and totally charming.

She wound up the flex and carried the machine downstairs. The rain had settled in for the day now and she was glad she had returned the bicycle to the dimness of its home. Cleaning it and taking it for a test run was best left until another day.

★   ★   ★

Mark's visit came sooner than his grandmother expected.

There was an impatient ring on the doorbell as soon as the evening meal was finished and cleared away. Then the door into the kitchen burst open and a young man stood there in a crimson shirt and light green jacket, beaming at them both.

'Mark!'

'All right, then, Gram?'

'As right as I'll ever be,' Jane said tartly. 'Perhaps you can enlighten us.

Those bicycles in the store — have you any idea why there are so many?'

For a moment Mark looked blank and then he shrugged.

'No idea.' He turned to Katie, his dark eyes shining. 'Katie Robertson! I'd know you anywhere from what Rory said. He was spot on, although he didn't get the colour of your hair just right. You're ready?'

She glanced down at her old jersey and jeans.

'Ready for what?'

'I've had orders to collect you.'

Light dawned.

'Oh, you mean the quiz? But . . . '

'Explain yourself, Mark,' Jane said sharply. 'Why are you here?'

'I've got to be on my way, Gram, and fast. Are you coming with me or not, Katie? We don't want to be late and have them start without us, or we'll be in trouble. What d'you say?'

'Like this?'

'Why not? You look fine.'

Jane looked from one to the other.

'Is someone going to tell me what's going on?'

'There's a quiz down in town,' Katie said. 'I saw the nurse just as she was leaving this morning. She told me about it. I didn't know it was a definite arrangement.'

'That's Glenda for you,' Mark said. 'No stone left unturned.'

Katie smiled.

'She mentioned this person called Becky Tait but I'm sure you don't look a bit like her.'

'More handsome, wouldn't you say? And with better transport. Gram will vouch for my gentlemanly behaviour. Both hands on the steering wheel at all times. Isn't that so, Gram?' He bent and gave his grandmother a hug.

Jane let out a muted cry.

'Sorry!' he said, momentarily stricken.

'Don't worry, dear boy.' His grandmother patted his arm as if he was the one who needed comfort. 'Glenda, you say?'

She sounded satisfied.

'Well, Katie, my dear, what would you like to do?'

Katie hesitated.

'Should I leave you on your own?'

'I shall be fully occupied and quite happy.'

'Of course she will,' Mark said. 'But don't hang about.'

Katie wasn't at all sure she wanted to go with him but Mark had made the effort to come and it seemed churlish to refuse. Jane seemed eager for her to go, too.

The next moment, it seemed, she was in Mark's Volvo and he was negotiating the track in a way she found alarming.

'How are you getting on with the old girl, then?' Mark asked as he swerved out on to the road.

'Do you mean your grandmother?'

'If you say so.'

'I most certainly do. She's a lovely lady.'

He grinned.

'She is if you keep on the right side of her. She's pretty good at digging her heels in, you know. Don't say I didn't warn you.'

Not liking the way this conversation was going, Katie attempted to change the subject by asking about the evening ahead but didn't get any satisfactory answers. It appeared it was a normal kind of quiz — whatever that was — neither hard nor easy, but it was a good evening and apparently not to be missed.

The room at the rear of the building in town was an uproar of noise as they entered. A crowd of people were jostling at the bar and a few were seated at the tables. Teams of six were being organised and Katie found herself with five others who all looked in their early twenties or late teens. She was definitely out of her depth here.

This wasn't what Rory Hobson had had in mind when he sat there at the café table looking at her keenly and accusing her of being too young. Amongst this lot she felt positively ancient and wasn't at all sure of what she was doing here.

She had left Rory's grandmother alone up there at Jarrel Cottage. Suppose she had an accident and needed help and Katie wasn't there? The thought was unsettling.

Her companions were looking at her with interest, wanting to know how she came to be here when most of the visitors had gone home. She relaxed a little as she told them.

No-one commented on her leaving Jane on her own and as the evening wore on she began to enter into the spirit of it, with answers to some of the questions that surprised the other members of the team.

'How did you know that?' a young fresh-faced girl asked.

Katie smiled. No need to point out that her age was an asset when it came to general knowledge.

They didn't win but came a close second and she was glad she hadn't disgraced herself. Time had flown and she saw to her dismay that the clock on the wall announced that it was after ten and Mark showed no signs of moving.

She glanced at him over there in the corner with his arm round one girl and looking with interest at another. A fixture for the rest of the evening? It seemed like it.

She pulled her mobile out of her pocket and checked she had a signal, but the noise was too much in here to be able to hear anything. She got up to go outside.

'Hi,' she heard as she reached the door. 'Are you looking for a lift home?'

Katie smiled as she recognised the community nurse she had seen that morning. Glenda's beaming smile looked friendly. It was good to see a familiar face.

'I was about to phone for a taxi.'

'So Mark Hobson's otherwise engaged, is he? Well, I got you into this and it's only fair to get you out of it. Come on, my car's close by. I'm leaving anyway.'

Glenda got a flashlight from her bag and in its light Katie saw her vehicle round the corner next to Mark's Volvo. Other than themselves the street was empty.

'I was pleased to see you there tonight, Katie,' Glenda said as they left the last houses of the town behind them. 'Becky couldn't come but Mark offered to bring you.'

'I enjoyed it,' Katie said.

'It got you out, and that's good. Jane Hobson is a lot weaker than she thinks, between you and me. It's a question now of finding somewhere suitable for her.'

This was worrying.

'She's adamant that she won't leave her home, though,' Katie said. 'Are you sure that's the best option?'

'Mark could be anywhere, on or off the island and Rory's not here most of the time. She's a very persuasive lady but her grandsons are right to be worried.'

'Even Mark?' Katie said in surprise.

'Oh, yes, even Mark. He shows it in odd ways but deep down he's just as anxious as Rory. He needs a guiding hand, that's all.'

'I see.'

But Katie didn't really. What could a guiding hand do if he was determined to live life his way? From what she had seen of Mark so far he followed his own agenda and that seemed to include only himself and the latest girlfriend.

'And you, Katie?' Glenda said, her tone softening. 'You must look after your own wellbeing to be strong enough to cope with everything here. Don't forget that, will you? Your health matters, too.'

Katie smiled, thinking of something else that mattered to her. Even now, late as it was, Jane might still be poring over those photographs looking to find a hint of a likeness that would convince the two of them of something important.

7

Magic in the Air

Armed with a shopping list in Jane Hobson's neat handwriting, Katie made her way as directed to Jarrel Farm, the home of the Jane's younger grandson, Mark.

At breakfast Jane had sounded put out rather than worried when she said he hadn't called round to collect the list, as was his custom. If he didn't come himself he sent one of his employees instead.

She couldn't understand it. He had said nothing about it one way or the other last night.

'Would you like me to take it to him?' Katie had asked.

'Would you, dear? That would be kind. I'll telephone him and leave a message.'

Katie had expected the farm to be close by but Jane not only explained its situation but also drew a little map on the back of an envelope to show the way.

Katie set off down the potholed track, avoiding the puddles. She reached the road and turned right, past small fields bounded by hedges of what were rows of budding flowers she now knew she must always refer to as narcissi.

She paused once or twice to imagine how they would look in a few months' time, fields of shining gold in the sunshine. She hoped she would still be here to see them.

Fifteen minutes later she arrived at Jarrel farmyard. Five tall orange containers stood to one side and a heap of palettes. Awkwardly dumped rolls of wire netting were nearby and looked as if they had been there for ages, judging by the tufts of grass growing out of them.

Directly in front of her was a barn

and through the open doors Katie saw various items of machinery, piles of large and small boxes, a trestle table near the door with a bucket of bunches of tightly budded flowers and a bright yellow tin with a wide slot in it for money.

The building smelled vaguely of sawdust.

The place was deserted and she had time to take a closer look at the bunched stems held together by elastic bands. Most of the stems were tightly budded with one in each bunch showing a hint of colour, yellow in most cases but one or two were obviously a white variety. *Fifty pence a bunch*, the notice said. *A bargain*.

If she had brought money with her she would have purchased some and carried them back with her to Jarrel Cottage. But why weren't there some at the cottage already? She was still considering this when a truck swung into the yard and screeched to a halt.

The driver leaped out, looking full of

vibrant life in his bright shirt.

'Mark!'

She went outside again to greet him, blinking in the sunlight. He seemed years younger this morning, far too young to be in charge here. She had placed Rory in his mid to late thirties but in daylight Mark seemed hardly older than a schoolboy. Maybe it was his quick movements that gave the wrong impression.

'Hi, there.'

He seemed at ease as he greeted her in a voice full of warmth and energy. There was no apology for not being here to greet her, just a wave of his hand when someone came out from an inner door, paused and then said he would leave them to it.

'I was up extra early today,' he said, his voice vibrant with self-importance. 'A call from one of our flower outlets on the mainland. We deal with them personally.

'The narcissi order slipped my mind yesterday and they were frantic, I have to say. A wedding, you see, the day after

75

tomorrow and they'd ordered short-stems for the table decorations. I got them away, though, just in time. They'll be happy.'

She smiled, wondering what would have happened if someone else had been contacted instead and he'd lost the contract and probably more business in the future. The thought of that obviously hadn't occurred to Mark.

'Your grandmother . . . ' she began.

He clapped his hand to his forehead.

'Don't tell me she's frantic about her favourite grandson and thinks I've got myself into some unimaginable trouble after last night. Is that it?'

'She has a shopping list for you. Here.'

He stared at it as if he'd never seen handwriting before. Then he frowned.

'Why did you bring it?'

'Your grandmother was anxious about it,' she said. 'I offered.'

'So you came to check on me, is that it? Well, that makes a change from my cousin always on my case. He'll have told you how things stand with Gram? Getting the old girl out of that place could be the best thing we've done.'

'I feel privileged to be here looking after her interests.' How prim and patronising she sounded, Katie thought.

'Don't let her fool you. She's always trying to get someone on her side.'

She felt chilled by his reaction.

'Not at all.'

He shrugged, unconcerned. Already he seemed anxious to be off.

'I've got a lot on today.'

His condescending smile annoyed her. She took the list from him.

'Don't worry. I'll see to the shopping myself,' she said.

'If you're sure?' He held his head a little one side as he smiled at her again.

She nodded, not trusting herself to speak. It wasn't until she was well on her way back to the cottage that she calmed down.

She didn't doubt that Mark Hobson could do as his grandmother asked him, if he chose. She thought of Jane

Hobson's kindness and understanding to herself, a stranger.

And yet someone like that was blessed with grandsons who, it appeared, did little to consider her wishes.

Life was so unfair.

★ ★ ★

The taxi dropped Katie off in what seemed the centre of the small town. The grey building and the sea on both sides of it were her first impressions, with wheeling sea gulls overhead and the tangy scent of seaweed.

For a moment she felt out of her comfort zone but then she gave herself a mental shake and headed off down the narrow street as if she had been here a hundred times before.

A small plane flew low overhead, preparing to land at the airport. Today was one of days that the Co-op delivered and that was definitely a bonus.

Jane's list was easily dealt with. She'd told Katie that all she needed to do was to pack the items into her shopping bags, add her name and address and leave them in the trolley.

Another plane was roaring over when Katie emerged into the street, silver against the blue sky. On the other side away from the harbour she found a modern building that turned out to be the tourist office overlooking Porth-cressa beach.

The outgoing tide was exposing more rocks and the sand was silvery gold among the drift of brown seaweed.

She opened the door of the building and went inside. There were displays of leaflets covering all sorts of events taking place during the season. Katie picked up one that explained about the annual gig racing that looked interesting.

She looked at the stand of postcards and selected one to send to Anna. She took it to the desk and then noticed a pocket map of St Mary's that would be useful, and picked that up, too.

'Are you on holiday?' the assistant

asked with interest. 'It's a quiet time of year now.'

The phone rang before Katie had time to pay and she waited, half-listening to a one-sided conversation that sounded interesting.

'A wok?' the assistant said, her voice rising in surprise. 'No, we don't actually keep them here. This is the Tourist Office. Yes, you could bring your own. But why don't you check at the place where you'll be staying?

'Oh, I see. Yes, there's a hardware shop that sells most things. Well, no, there's not a specialist shop as well.'

She shrugged and raised her eyebrows at Katie as she put the phone down.

'It takes all sorts.'

'Woks Are Us?' Katie suggested.

The next moment both had dissolved into giggles.

The assistant wiped her eyes and took Katie's money. Katie liked her soft grey hair, tied back from a cheerful face by a band of yellow ribbon.

She noticed the badge she was wearing, that hadn't shown up at first on her white fluffy cardigan, and saw that the woman was *Miss Marcia Fletcher*.

'Tell me,' Marcia said with a twinkle in her eyes, 'you don't want to know if we use Euros as our currency here, do you, or what to do for food since you can't bring your car over here laden to the gunnels?'

Katie smiled.

'Not this time, but I'll know who to contact if I do.'

'Of course, they're the exceptions, you understand. We love it when people come back year after year. It's such a special place, you see.'

Katie explained her own position and then listened to a glowing account of Jane Hobson who, it seemed, had once been active in the town after her retirement, and had become involved with the charity shop as well as working in the tourist office on a regular basis.

'There isn't much she doesn't know

about the islands,' Katie was told. 'A wonderful lady from an old Scilly family. I'm still sorry my niece and Jane's grandson decided to split up.

'Tansy's fault, I suspect, though they said it was mutual. She's off backpacking round Australia now as happy as anything.'

The assistant nodded as she picked up a duster and wiped the counter clean of imaginary dust.

'Rory's a fine young man. He takes after his grandmother, both of them with that strong sense of family. I like that.'

They talked a little longer and then Katie went outside into the breezy air that stirred the few palm trees on the promenade. There were places to sit to shelter and she was glad to stay there for some time admiring the golden sparkle on the sea and the strange formation of rocks on the tip of the headland to the left.

She had time to write the postcard to Anna, too.

When she had done that she sat for a moment more gazing over the sea to the headland on the right, deep in thought.

Back there in the tourist office the assistant had described Rory as a lovely young man. Not even his grandmother had called him that and it wasn't the first adjective that would have sprung to her own mind in describing Rory Hobson to a stranger.

Anna, Katie thought, would be glad to hear it.

It was easy to feel the magic in the air. Scilly was a good place to be, especially as she was needed here. Even though Jane Hobson wasn't aware that she had admitted her vulnerability to anyone.

8

Close Encounter

Katie hadn't dared venture out on the bicycle yet. She needed to clean and oil it first and to take a test run to make sure all was working as it should.

But first there was the housework to see to, especially the bedrooms which, apart from making Jane's bed each morning, she had ignored on Jane's insistence. Jane had pointed out that Rory had arranged a thorough spring-clean upstairs only a day or two before Katie arrived.

Glenda was her usual cheerful self when she called in to change Jane's dressings, even though she was in a hurry to reach her next patient and wouldn't even pause for a quick coffee.

'I'm off to Blanchards' place now. They're short of pickers there, I think, now Jim's had his accident. The flower farmers are having a tough time with all this warm weather on the mainland. See you!'

And she was off.

Puzzled, Katie carried the vacuum cleaner upstairs. Mark Hobson had seemed cheerful enough when she had called at the farm but what did she know?

Most people she had encountered down in town had seemed pleased with the warmth so late in the season, and she had seen one or two trailers on the backs of vehicles containing the bunched narcissi on the way to the airport.

Rory had said in the advert that she would have the chance to work as a picker if she desired. Katie would make a point of checking out books on the flower industry at the library as soon as she could.

The chance to sort the bicycle out came the next afternoon when she had settled Jane for her afternoon rest. Katie wheeled the machine out into the sunlight, leaned it against the wall of the building and set to work. It took longer than she expected but by the time she had finished it looked respectable enough and at least the rust wasn't quite as bad as it had been. Cleaning herself up afterwards and checking on Jane took almost as long but at last she was ready.

Taking great care, she set off down the track to the road. She wobbled a little at first but by the time she got to the end of the track she felt decidedly more confident. She rode back to the cottage, enjoying the sensation of the wind in her hair and the feeling that she was no longer reliant on her own two feet to get about or on the kindness of others.

Then she turned the bicycle round and headed for the road again, swerving round the potholes and feeling as masterful as Glenda must have done as she whipped along here in her little car.

This time, though, she was more adventurous and set off along the empty road to the right. She had time to notice some pickers in one of the bulb fields, bent low over their tasks, before she was past and approaching the bend in the road that went steeply downhill.

She pulled hard on the brake and then, in panic, the other one at the same time. The next moment she was pitching over the handlebars in front of an oncoming car. It swerved and stopped.

For a frightening moment Katie struggled to breathe. Then she felt herself lifted into an upright position.

'Wait!' a voice commanded. Rory's? 'Keep still.'

His arms held her close to him for the few moments it took for the air to come back to her lungs. The strength of his body as she leaned against him comforted her for a blessed moment of relief.

Then humiliation flooded in.

'I didn't mean . . . ' she started to say, but the words wouldn't come.

She was breathing normally now but he said nothing as he released her. She watched him move the bicycle to one side and lean it against the bank where his car had landed up moments before.

As he turned she dare not look at him. Over-confidence had led to this and it was her fault. The bike was damaged but her pride even more so.

'Are you hurt?' he said.

'I was winded, that's all, thank you.'

'Your knee.'

She looked down at it and saw the rip in the right knee of her jeans and a gaping hole in the other with blood glistening through it. Her shoulders ached and she was trembling.

'It's all right, it's only . . . '

'Anything broken? You're standing awkwardly. A check-up at the hospital would be wise.'

'No!' She was horrified. 'I'm feeling bruised, that's all.' She flexed her wrists and ankles to check and then stood upright to prove there was nothing seriously wrong.

He looked at her closely.

'You're sure? Then I'll drive you home.'

Home? How long would Jarrel Cottage be home to her after this? Mortified, she said nothing as he lifted the bicycle into the boot of his car. She was in no position to argue as he opened the passenger door of his car for her to get in.

He turned to look at her when he was seated. His face was pale and the lines round his mouth had deepened. In shame she knew that the shock he was feeling must be as deep as her own. Only swift action on his part had prevented something much worse.

'I'd rather my grandmother doesn't see you like this,' he said as he put the car into gear. 'She's supposed to be kept free of stress and this isn't the best way to go about it.'

Katie's hand shook as she fastened her safety belt.

'I'm sorry,' she said humbly.

'What possessed you to fly round that bend so quickly? You could have been killed. Have you no brakes on that bike? I take it you checked they were in working order? It's as well I was going slowly.'

He was right, of course. A drop of oil on the brakes, especially the stiff back one, and there would have been no problem. Another black mark against her.

She hung her head and stuttered out some excuse that she knew sounded weak.

They swept past the turning to Jarrel Cottage.

'Where are we going?'

'We have plenty of time to get you cleaned up at my place. No doubt my grandmother is resting. When does she expect you back?'

'There's no time limit.'

'Does she know that you've gone off on the bike?'

'She thought it was a good idea, that it would give me some independence.'

'Independence!' The scorn in his voice was evident. 'My grandmother would approve of that, of course. Independence is a quality she respects above all others. And that, of course, is the problem.'

'But how can it be a problem when there is someone living in with her?'

'She's weaker than she thinks, that's all. She needs care.'

He slowed down to round a bend. Here the road was narrower and he didn't gain speed again until they had passed the Old Town turning.

'She's in denial, of course,' he said then.

Katie thought of the care that Jane took not to do anything heavy or onerous. She had thought it was because of the operation but now she saw that it was something more than that, even if her grandsons didn't think so.

'She's not stupid,' she said.

Ignoring that, he fixed his gaze on the road.

'That's why a more experienced person would be more suitable as a companion, someone who perhaps has had experience of these things and isn't afraid of the responsibility.'

His assumption that she wasn't that person was humiliating. At any other time she would have lashed out, given as good as she got and left him in no doubt that his grandmother wouldn't be better off by having someone she disapproved of moving in with her. But this strange weakness was debilitating.

'I love looking after her,' was all she could manage to say.

She could see he didn't believe her. He probably thought she was here for her own motives, like a holiday on these beautiful islands and the desire to get it on the cheap. But then her indignation faded. He was right, of course, she was here for her own reasons — even if they were different from those he'd imagined.

At the same time she had become very fond of Jane and could understand her feelings of outrage at being treated like an object. A lack of choice, that was it. The feeling that you were a nuisance to everyone else. Jane must be the one to make the decision as to her future whatever that may be. Respect was lacking here.

Katie was beginning to feel cold now and too weak, too hazy to think straight. She slumped forward, her eyes closed. She felt the car slow down and stop. She opened her eyes to see boats lined up on the area of grass in front of her. She recognised it as one end of Porthcressa beach.

'We're here,' he said.

He helped her out of the car. She could see the sand now and the group of houses and cottages on the other side, their white fronts illuminated in the sunshine.

The tide was out and areas of brown seaweed glistened among the sand. The sharp scent of salt and tar wasn't there today, though, or perhaps she was incapable of noticing it.

Rory's home was the end one of three cottages, each with a small walled garden in front. His was overgrown with straggling shrubs. He opened the unlocked front door for her to go ahead of him. He hadn't locked his car door either, she noted. Perhaps these things didn't matter here.

Rory ushered her into the kitchen at the front and she was aware of light and space and warmth. The scent of herbs was pleasant, too. He plugged in a kettle and then pulled a chair in front of the Aga for her. There was a round wooden table and chairs painted white to match the cupboard beneath the window.

'The bathroom's through there,' he said, indicating a door in the corner. 'You'll find all you need in the wall cabinet. See you in a few moments. A hot drink next, I think. I'll have it ready.'

Her grazed knee wasn't as bad as she had thought from the amount of blood, and was soon dealt with. An extra-wide sticking plaster was useful since there was a gap in her jeans and applying it made her feel more respectable. She doused her face in cold water and found a comb in her pocket to tidy her hair.

The tea Rory made was strong and she attempted to drink it scalding hot, but then put the mug down on the table.

He smiled as he drew up a chair nearby.

'Too hot?'

'Just a little.'

She felt a lot more human now and warmth flooded her cheeks at the gentle tone in his voice. He sounded as if he cared yet just now, as they swept down the road into Hugh Town, he had been harsh and unforgiving.

Rightly so, of course, in the circumstances. But a little sympathy would have been good.

She picked up her cup again and took an exploratory sip. The time she had been away from the cottage couldn't have been much more than three quarters of an hour but felt a lot longer. So much had happened in a short time.

Suddenly she thought of something, reminded by the book lying on the dresser with a picture of bulb fields on the cover.

'Glenda said something I didn't understand,' she said hesitantly.

'About my grandmother?' Some tea slopped on to the table as Rory put his mug down hurriedly.

'No, no,' she said, seeing his concern. 'About flower farming.'

'And that was?'

'She said the farmers were having tough time with all this warm weather on the mainland.'

'Think about it.'

'It's warm here, as well. Oh, I see!'

It wasn't rocket science to work that one out and she was glad she hadn't wasted much time in doing so.

'The cost of the travel from here to the mainland is the problem if the market's being flooded from elsewhere and makes a huge dent in any profits.'

'You'll make an economist yet.'

He leaned back in his seat, smiling at her. It was a lovely moment she didn't want to end but there was Jane to think of and time was moving on.

'I should get back.'

'Tired of my company already?'

'Your grandmother . . . '

'She knows you're here. She's fine.' From the shelf at his side he picked up his mobile phone. 'Wonderful things these.'

He slipped it in his pocket and stood up.

'Finish your tea first and while you're doing it I'll remove the bike.'

'Oh.' She had forgotten the bike.

'It needs some attention but it's not much damaged. I'll work on it before I go off and drop it back at Jarrel Cottage.'

'That's kind but . . . '

'I'll be outside when you're ready to go.'

She did as he said, wondering for the first time where he had been going when she careered round the bend. To visit his grandmother, she supposed. So he'd see Jane only a little later than planned.

She carried her empty cup across to the sink, hesitated about washing it up and decided to leave it on the draining board.

At the door she noticed a row of brass hooks nearby with two jackets hanging there, both of them fairly new.

One of them was a dull olive green. The other was pink.

Katie opened the door and went out.

9

Planning Ahead

At Jarrel Cottage Rory managed to give Katie time to slip upstairs and change into her new jeans, unseen by Jane. He was gone when she came down again, off on some important business, Jane told her.

'You're looking pale, dear,' she added as she sat down in her usual place on the sofa.

Jane's rest this afternoon could only have been a short one, Katie thought. The cushions were still disturbed and the crocheted blanket she used to cover herself had slipped to the floor.

Katie picked it up and folded it and then rubbed at her cheeks in the hope her normal colour would spring back into them.

'Sit down, Katie. Just rest for a little

while and you'll soon feel better. Delayed shock needs looking after.'

Katie did as she said, touched by her thoughtfulness. Shock? She should have got over that ages ago.

It was only a fall from a bike and there had been somebody there to pick her up and brush her off. Someone with strong arms, she thought with a shiver of recollection, whose body as he held her against him until her breath flooded back had felt strong and protective.

Not only that but he had been kindness itself when he had taken her back to his place so she could recover a little and wash the wound in her knee. He had showed a concern for her as well as for his grandmother that she would never have suspected.

Jane looked at her from over her glasses.

'There are four more bicycles in the barn,' she said.

Katie gazed at her in surprise.

'Rory told you what happened?'

'He said that you'd had a bit of a fall,

100

that's all. It happens.'

'I suppose so.'

But not quite like that, Katie thought. Not by throwing herself in the path of an oncoming car because she was unable to slow down.

'It was my own stupid fault. I'll be more careful next time.'

'So there will be a next time?'

'Oh, yes.'

Katie smiled as she saw the twinkle in Jane's eyes. Jane wasn't a person to give up easily and neither was she. They had that in common, even if no likeness had turned up so far in any of the photographs.

There were other avenues to explore and soon she would think about them.

Jane's realisation that something had happened to the bicycle was uncanny. At this rate she would be able to explain how the pink jacket came to be hanging on the hook in Rory's kitchen.

In spite of herself, the image stuck in Katie's mind. Stop it! She ought to shove it to the back of her mind and get on with something useful, like tidying the pile of albums on the small table in front of Jane. She would make sure that the one on top was still open at the page Jane had been studying.

She had thought of suggesting to Jane that she might like an outing with her if the weather held, perhaps by taxi down to Hugh Town or any other part of the island she wished to visit.

But now, after Rory's talk of Jane's increasing weakness, she was glad she hadn't mentioned it, because first she must check with Glenda that it was a good idea.

'You're looking thoughtful, dear. Are you feeling better now?'

'Me? Oh, yes, thank you.'

Jane struggled to her feet and reached for her stick.

'Then perhaps a walk in the fresh air will do us both some good.'

'Are you sure? Rory said — '

'Rory?' Jane said in scorn. 'Does he not think I know how to look after myself?'

She had reached the door by this time and Katie, smiling, shrugged.

'Just a little way then,' she said.

They didn't venture far, just past the place where the track turned to lead down to the coast path. They soon came to the wooden seat placed where there was a good view of the sea and islands.

'This is your time off,' Jane said, settling herself comfortably, 'so don't let me keep you, my dear. I'm quite happy sitting here and there's plenty more for you to see further on.'

'I'm happy here as well,' Katie said as she sat down, too.

With her shoulders still aching, walking further on to reach the coast path definitely didn't appeal.

They sat in silence for a while and then, when it was time to go, Katie got to her feet gingerly, having stiffened up in the short time they had been sitting here.

They walked slowly up to the sharp turn in the track.

Jane paused and pointed ahead with her stick.

'Jarrel Farm is quite close to where we are now,' she said. 'Can you see? There was a path through here once. We used to come down this way most mornings when I was a child, just to check that the sea was still there.'

'And was it?'

'Not always. Not when the sea mist came in and blotted everything out. We loved it then, too, with everything so silent and mysterious.'

'You lived at Jarrel Farm?'

Jane nodded.

'The path was wider then, of course. You could get a vehicle down it quite easily. The fields down below were good bulb fields. I used to help sometimes with the picking.'

Now that she was looking closely Katie could see signs that there had once been a way between hedges that had been allowed to deteriorate into practically nothing.

In places stunted hawthorn remained

but the grass and dead brambles did a good job of disguising what used to be a thoroughfare of sorts.

'It could be opened up again, surely?'

'Mark likes his cars,' Jane said, 'and the road is handy. You can see that it hasn't been used for years.'

Katie could hardly make it out, but it had given her an idea. As far as she could see the land was flat here, with none of the steep slopes up and down in the other directions. A proper path would mean that Jane could take little walks this way if she chose.

'It would make a good shortcut to the farm on foot, wouldn't it?' she said. 'I'd like to do some flower picking, in my free time, of course.'

Suddenly she knew that this was something she really wanted to do if Mark would agree. She could find out about borrowing some shears and set to work on the undergrowth as soon as her aches and pains had disappeared.

On the short way back to the cottage Jane told her a little of what it was like to be out there in the bulb fields in all weathers, bending over for hours and hours. It sounded hard work but the nostalgia Katie heard in her voice was touching.

And yet there were no narcissi in the cottage, scenting the air, she thought.

At the garden gate Katie reached forward to unlatch it and gave an exclamation of pain she tried to smother.

'My dear, you are hurt?'

'No, really, it's nothing. It'll pass off.'

'I think we should contact Glenda and see what she says.'

Katie was horrified.

'On her day off?'

'She works at weekends sometimes. I'll see what I can do.'

'No, no, please.'

But Jane, ignoring her, let the gate snap shut behind her and went resolutely to the door.

There was nothing that Katie say or do apart from cutting the phone wires to stop her from telephoning. Rory had described his grandmother as stubborn.

She could see now what he meant.

Please, please let Glenda be out!

'No, dear, it's not me,' she heard Jane say. 'It's Katie. Yes. She had a fall from her bike and doesn't look too good. You could? I'm grateful and she will be, too, if her shoulder turns out to need treatment. Half an hour? We'll expect you.'

In the brief time Jane was setting her up for something that wasn't necessary, Katie glanced round the room and in her mind's eye furnished it with bed and chest of drawers. It would make a fine bedroom for Jane so that she didn't have to climb the stairs. One day she would make it happen. Jane wasn't going to have everything her own way!

* * *

'Young Mark Hobson's taken on a bit of a challenge, I'll say that for him,' Glenda said. Her broad smile and relaxed pose as she reclined in one of the easy chairs made Jane and Katie smile too.

Glenda had arrived only a minute or two after the promised 30 minutes, wearing jeans and a bright orange top and hiking boots. For a moment Katie hadn't recognised her, although she had seen her out of uniform on the night of the quiz.

Gone was the slightly formal manner and her smile was friendly even though it was obvious that Jane's concern about the shoulder was unfounded.

'I was going to call in anyway,' she said. 'On foot this time. A social call, of course, and thanks for the tea.'

She put her empty cup down on the low table that Katie had cleared of the photograph albums.

Her examination of Katie's shoulder had taken only minutes. Satisfied, Jane had accepted her verdict that nothing was broken and was now talking about her younger grandson.

'I was doing a walk round the island,' Glenda said, 'the northern bit this time and I came round past Jarrel Farm. I see Mark's got some holiday accommodation advertised. Branching out a bit, isn't he?'

'He's been making plans,' Jane said. 'I have nothing to do with it.'

'Good luck to him.'

'Katie's been talking about doing some picking for him,' Jane said. 'I tell her it's back-breaking work in all weathers.'

Katie, smiling, tried to wiggle her shoulders but gave a grimace of pain.

'So he's needing help now, is he?'

'I don't know yet,' Katie said, 'but there's no harm in finding out. I'll see what he says and borrow some tools.

'I want to get cracking on cutting back the undergrowth on the path from the cottage to the farm. That way it'll take me not much more than five minutes to get there on foot.'

'Not on your bike?'

There was something in Glenda's voice that alerted Katie to the nurse's underlying amusement, although her expression was serious.

'Probably not,' Katie said.

'Rather you than me. That path's been unused for years. It'll take some doing.'

Katie was aware of that. She might have to wait a little before she got going on it.

A gentle walk round by road tomorrow afternoon was probably all she could manage with any discomfort.

10

Disturbing Message

Again Jarrel Farm resembled a ghost farm when Katie got there on Sunday afternoon. Mark had said he would be around — so where was he?

The yard looked just as untidy as on her last visit. The barn door stood wide open as usual but just inside was a board with a colourful poster attached leaning against the table that held the narcissi container and the money tin.

Intrigued, Katie went inside for a closer look. The tractor was here and the small truck with its trailer but there was no sign of the car.

The information on the poster was brief and to the point. There were two new properties on offer as holiday lets with a mobile phone number for more details.

If Mark had shears they were not in evidence among the muddle of tools and equipment at the end of the building. Katie was wasting her time looking. It made more sense to ring the bell on the door of the house to alert him that she was here.

No reply. She wandered back out through the yard to the road and hesitated. Since she was here it might be an idea to find the start of the path between here and the cottage from this side. At first glance, though, it seemed impossible.

Then Katie saw that in one place the brambles were a little thinner than those on either side and there were a few stones which might once have been a wall.

It seemed likely that she had found it, but if anything the riot of undergrowth was in a worse state than the cottage end. No-one would have dreamed it was once a well-used track such as Jane had described.

Deep in thought, Katie didn't hear

the car and was startled to find Mark approaching her on foot across the yard. He looked, in his bright clothes, as if he'd just returned from some exotic holiday. Impossible, of course, as no planes were flying today. Impossible, too, for a flower farmer to leave his work at this important time of year.

But she had the feeling that nothing would prevent Mark doing something his heart was set on, if push came to shove.

'A last-minute appointment,' Mark said breathlessly, smiling at her with his head held a little to one side.

The thought passed through her mind that someone must once have told him how engaging he looked when he did this.

His apparent delight in seeing her didn't falter, either.

'Your grandmother said there was once a way through here,' Katie said.

'You'd have to be a raging bull to get through now.'

She laughed and he laughed with her.

'I'm really sorry I wasn't here,' he said.

'Have you some secateurs I could borrow, or shears, perhaps? I'd like to have a go at clearing a way through.'

'Sounds crazy to me. There's a scythe, a really sharp one. Might do the trick. It'd be too heavy for you to use, though.' Again that charming smile. 'I might get it for you once the next Sol order is off. That won't be for the next day or two.'

'Are you still needing someone to pick for you?' she said.

He looked startled.

'Has Rory said anything?'

'Should he have?'

'Don't tell me you haven't noticed that he likes his say in anything and everything?'

When she said nothing he shrugged and indicated they should cross the lane to look at one of the small hedged fields on the other side. She felt a stirring of excitement as they leaned on the wooden gate.

'All those rows and rows of plants,' she said. 'Daffodils . . . narcissi, I mean. All in bud and looking as if they're about to burst into bloom, and it's only November.'

He laughed.

'It's the season over here. We pick them in bud like this and send them off to the mainland. Soleil d'Or. They're the tazetas, the early ones.'

'It sounds like a foreign language,' she said.

'Have you done anything like it before?'

'Never.'

'You'll get used to it.'

She nodded. They moved back towards the house and as they did so Mark waved his hand towards what looked at first like some outhouses attached to the back of the building.

As she followed him closer she saw that there were windows and doors. It seemed that one stood open but she couldn't be sure because of the huge pile of netting and various objects stacked in front.

'Holiday cottages,' he said with pride. 'Like to take a look inside?'

Her first thought was that the high hedge of pittosporum close by hid what view there might have been. The next was that they looked unfinished. But Mark's satisfaction in the properties was evident.

The cramped rooms, all on one floor, were furnished after a fashion. But the kitchen had no decent flooring, only coarse matting that felt uneven beneath her feet.

There was the smell of new paint and of disinfectant, and the wall cupboards of startling red didn't quite match the crimson cupboards beneath.

He seemed not to notice her silence in his confidence that this project was going to make his fortune.

'I like colour,' he said with satisfaction. 'Two bedrooms. Like to take a look?'

Each was too small to contain more than a small double bed and a chair.

No wonder she had had to squeeze past a small wardrobe in the passage, she thought. Surely one bedroom of a decent size would have been far more sensible?

Outside, Mark glanced at his watch and she could see he was impatient to be off.

'Like a lift?' he said. 'I can drop you at the end of the lane if you like.'

It seemed impolite to refuse and they set off, his foot hard down on the accelerator. As they swept along, the thought crossed Katie's mind that if she had met him at the bend yesterday when she was on the bicycle her chance of survival might have been slim.

He drew up at the lane junction and she got out. He turned the car with admirable skill, waited to see in which direction she decided to go, gave a wave and drove back the way they had come.

So he'd just wanted her off the premises, and quickly, too. So hurriedly, in fact, that he had forgotten why she had come. Katie was no further knowing if, and when, he wanted her to start work as a picker or if he had cutting tools he was prepared to lend her.

★ ★ ★

For some reason Katie didn't want Jane to know the result of her visit to the farm this afternoon so she was relieved when her assistance was required in locating a bag of embroidery wool that Jane had put in a safe place, and then forgotten exactly where that place was.

When it was at last located — in the airing cupboard, out of sight behind a pile of folded towels — Jane could think only of the pattern she had invented and wanted to try out.

Only later when they were having an early tea at the kitchen table did she remember Katie's plans. By then Katie could think of Mark only with amusement and was able to make a good story of it.

'He'll be after you as soon as he

remembers your offer to help with the picking,' Jane said with confidence. 'And if he isn't we'll do something about it ourselves. Mark's not like Rory.

'Did I tell you Rory dropped your bike off while you were out? It's keeping the others company in the barn.'

'So your rest was interrupted again today?'

'Not a bit of it. Mark would have rushed straight in with never a thought, but not Rory. He left as quietly as he came and I didn't see him. There were two notes on the doormat when I awoke. One of them for you, of course. It's there on the dresser.'

Katie gazed across at it and then got up reluctantly. His writing was large and strong-looking. A notice of dismissal? Surely not.

But why should he find a written communication necessary? There was only one way to find out, of course. She ripped the envelope open.

Inside was a sheet of thick white

paper with a business address, phone numbers and an e-mail address at the top. In even larger handwriting halfway down were two words.

TAKE CARE!

She smiled, replaced it in the envelope and slipped it in her pocket.

11

Always on Her Mind

Late on Tuesday morning Katie set off for town on the bicycle that Rory had repaired for her. Jane needed a prescription to be collected at the health centre. Katie also planned a visit to the library to borrow suitable books on flower farming and researching family history, and to enquire about classes that might help. Jane thought this an excellent idea.

There was something about speed in the open air that Katie loved. The wind in her hair, the way the bulb fields flashed past and the knowledge that the brakes on the bike were in tip-top condition and totally reliable were wonderful.

Downhill most of the way, what could be better — especially as her aches and pains were almost things of the past? She would worry about the uphill ride back when the time came.

She arrived at the Strand with glowing face and ruffled hair and stopped for a moment to breathe in the salty air from the beach and to admire the harbour boats and the open sea beyond with the off-islands in the distance.

There was time to tidy her hair and to look round for a good place to leave the bike.

'Anywhere will do,' Jane had told her. 'You can leave it where you like. It'll be quite safe.'

Jane's prescription took priority, of course, but once that was collected Katie was free to wander round the small town and do as she pleased. She paused on seeing a craft fair advertised on the town hall notice board for the following Saturday week. It would take place at Bolrice Farm.

She memorised the details with the

thought of Jane's handiwork in mind.

After that it was the hardware shop to ask about buying shears. The idea of owning her own had come to her on her ride down into town, reminded by the bulb fields she passed. Waiting for Mark to do something about it was a waste of good bramble-shearing time. Perhaps it was a foolish idea but it was something she wanted to do.

The sound of Rory's voice behind her sent shivers through her. She spun round.

'There's nothing wrong at the cottage, is there?'

She shook her head.

'Should there be?'

He eyed the shears in her hand.

'You do know a mobile hairdresser visits my grandmother every now and again?'

Her lips twitched.

'She told me.'

'Who's with her now?'

'Glenda arrived as I left, if it's any business of yours. Well, I suppose it is.

Sorry.' She had spoken without thinking and he didn't deserve her rebuke.

She owed him more of an explanation as well as thanks for repairing her bicycle.

'Glenda brought a friend of your grandmother's with her.'

'A friend?'

'Enid. Jane was pleased to see her. They were at school together years ago.'

He nodded but still looked doubtful.

'It took me all of seven minutes to get down here,' she said, exasperated at his reaction, 'and it won't be much more to get back. We don't need to worry that they'll be at each other's throats.'

He nodded.

'Where did you leave the bike?'

'Thanks for bringing it back in such good condition, by the way. It's on the Strand.'

'Admiring the view?'

'Wishing it was amphibious.'

'It wants to explore another island?'

'Who wouldn't?'

'I've arranged to go over to St

Martin's in a day or two to see a client over there. I could take it with me in the hired boat, if you like?'

Katie pretended to consider.

'We don't like to be apart, you see.'

'Then that poses a problem.'

'Regretfully, yes.'

She smiled at him in challenge. His frequent assumptions that she wasn't doing her job properly were beginning to get to her.

'Then I shall have to work on it.' His tone was pleasant but then he frowned. 'You'll have a problem carrying your purchase back with you since there's no saddle bag on the bike.'

'Not at all,' she said promptly. 'It's all arranged.'

Until that moment she hadn't thought how it could be done but she wasn't going to admit that, or allow him to take the shears back to Jarrel Cottage for her.

Her next visit this morning would be to the sports shop for a suitable rucksack to carry on her back. She could do with one anyway.

She took the shears to the pay desk near the door. She didn't look back as she left the shop, walking purposely away until she knew she was out of sight.

Once out of town it was a long drag that seemed unending. Proud of herself for not giving in and getting off and pushing the bike up the steepest part, she took the shears straight into the barn.

It was only then that she remembered she hadn't visited the library. As well as borrowing books on flower farming she had intended making enquiries about researching family history and perhaps booking time on one of the computers for setting about it online.

Oh, well, another time. Blame Rory Hobson for that with his obvious distrust of her and the way she was doing her job. It was enough to send everything else out of her mind.

★ ★ ★

As they had a guest for lunch Katie was going to suggest that she lay the table in the sitting-room. But Jane had spread out several beautiful patchwork quilts in there for her friend's inspection and there was an open box of what looked like embroidered cushion covers standing nearby, some of them spilling out.

A few other bags of assorted work were there, too. Enid very nearly overbalanced into the largest of them as she turned suddenly on Katie's entrance.

'Silly me!' she cried, laughing.

'That's Enid's work,' Jane told her when she saw Katie looking at it. 'Beautiful stuff and all kept hidden away like most of mine.

'But it needn't be,' Katie said. 'What about displaying it at the craft fair at Bolrice Farm on Saturday week, wherever that is?'

'You know about that?' Enid said, surprised.

'There's a poster down in town.'

Jane started to fold one of the quilts

and, smiling, Enid helped her.

'I've been thinking about it,' she said. 'We used to have them regularly years ago, didn't we, Jane? Remember those chair backs you sold? And I did a good line in dressing-table sets. It's high time there was another.'

'But do people want those sort of things these days?' Jane was doubtful.

She had a point, Katie thought.

Enid laughed.

'We've moved on a bit since then, haven't we? We were Enid Grant and Jane Abbott in those days. We've a lot to show now between the two of us. And that's what it'll be, an exhibition as well as a sale.'

'Out of season with the visitors all gone?'

'Not long before Christmas, though. Christmas presents, the very thing.'

Katie left them deep in discussion and went thoughtfully out to the kitchen.

Jane Abbott? Of course. It simply hadn't registered with her before that

Jane hadn't always been Jane Hobson. Hannah Jane Hobson. Her sneaking feeling that amongst the photographs in the albums there might be a resemblance between the younger Jane and herself was mere fantasy and wasn't going to happen.

In any case, being able to prove a family link to the Hobson family on Scilly was a difficult task with practically nothing to go on.

A sampler, that was all, worked by a young girl in 1860 with the same surname as Katie's mother; a common one when all was said and done.

Smiling at her folly, Katie opened a kitchen drawer to pull out a bright tablecloth. Enid's daughter would be here to collect her before long and they needed to eat, so out here it would have to be.

*　*　*

Becky Tait was the opposite of her short and bouncy mother. Her tall elegance in neat jeans and sweatshirt gave the impression of calm efficiency, while Enid's flowing clothes and flurry of upset bags and lost keys turned their departure into a major operation.

Jane sat on her sofa watching the proceedings through the open door. She obviously knew the score, Katie thought, as did Becky, who raised an eyebrow in amusement at Katie as the two of them stood together while Enid picked up one of the bags, looked at it and put it down again.

'Exhausting, isn't it?' Becky said, her lips twitching. 'Poor Mother just can't help herself. She drives Bob, my husband, mad.'

Katie smiled in sympathy. She could just imagine what a craft fair would be like with Enid's chaotic input.

'She lives with you?'

'On and off when she feels like it. She can't keep still for a minute. Off to the mainland touting her wares at markets over there. We store all her craft stuff. There's plenty of room. We have the farm down the road towards Old Town.'

'A flower farm?' Katie said.

'You're interested?'

'Very much so. Fascinated, is more the word.'

'Then come and visit us, why don't you, and I'll show you round? Phone first, though, to check we're free. Sometimes there's a mammoth order we have to attend to. But we'd love to see you at any other time. Liberty Farm. You can't miss it. Ready at last, Mother?'

'Ready and waiting,' Enid said. She beamed at Katie and Jane and they were off.

Later, wielding the new pair of shears, Katie started to hack her way through the obstructive undergrowth on the hidden path Jane had pointed out to her. There wasn't much of the afternoon left but perhaps that was a good thing, since she could stop this back-breaking job all the sooner and continue another day.

The trick was to concentrate her

thoughts on something else. Jane's grandsons, for instance — cousins but so different from each other.

Mark, so anxious to prove he could run the family flower farm successfully and yet lacking the ability for hard work and forward planning.

And then Rory ... Yes, Rory, watching her every move and causing her heart to plummet when he was near. Grow up, for goodness sake, she thought.

Don't let him get to you.

She paused and sat back on her heels for a brief rest. Then, noticing a particularly resistant piece of ivy, she attacked it with added vigour.

12

Avoiding Rory

The black clouds looming to the west looked ominous. By the time Katie was ready to set off after lunch for Liberty Farm drops of heavy rain were already bouncing on the porch roof when she opened the front door.

Becky had been enthusiastic when she telephoned after breakfast today.

'I'm free this afternoon,' she said, 'and the girls are here doing the bunching. Perfect.'

What wasn't so perfect was the change in the weather. No cycling down there in this downpour. A walk would be better as it wasn't far and Jane had offered her large black umbrella.

She had made no suggestion that Katie might like to postpone her visit. Allowing the weather to rule your life was not an option here, apparently. Unless you were hoping to get to the mainland, of course.

It had become second nature to listen for the sound of planes taking off at certain times and Katie realised that she hadn't heard the familiar roar for the last couple of hours.

Clad in Jane's voluminous waterproof cape, Katie set off down the track. It seemed as if the wild garlic still in bloom on the banks and the few late red campion flowers had given in to the weather. There was a stream of water at the side of the road now that became wider on the bend where another track joined it.

There came the sound of a vehicle behind her and, very carefully, a tractor and small trailer swished past her. She saw boxes full of narcissi all in bud. By the tyre marks in the mud as she reached the turning to Liberty Farm she knew that this was its destination, too.

There was movement inside the large

open doors of a barn and Katie went inside.

The trailer, disconnected from its tractor, was in the barn, too. Some of the boxes had been carried into an inside room where Katie could see the backs of two girls hard at work slipping elastic bands on bunches of flowers.

The background music was pleasant. She recognised the waltz from 'The Merry Widow', one of her dad's favourites.

At that moment Becky Tait appeared, beaming at her. Even in jeans and tattered pullover she looked elegant.

'Let's have your wet things, Katie,' she said. 'Coffee? I should think you need it. Good of you to come out in this.'

She spread the cape over some handy boxes and the jacket over the handle of a mower.

'Other people are out in it,' Katie said, glancing at the trailer.

'Oh, the pickers. They work all weathers, come rain or shine. They're a good bunch and we're lucky to have them since it's difficult to get hold of many this season. Come and meet the girls.'

There was an electric fire in one corner of the inner room and the warmth from it was welcome.

Helen and Abby, smiling a welcome, made the coffee for the four of them. There were two stools for Becky and Katie to perch on. The girls returned to their places by the bench that ran on two sides of the room where they had been bunching the narcissi and storing them in the box at their feet.

'Are they always placed upright like that?' Katie asked.

'Not always,' Becky said. 'Some are packed flat in boxes. When they come in from the fields the flowers are stored in the cold room in baskets called procona. And they stand in containers with water at their base. I'll show you in a minute when we've drunk our coffee.'

There were so many questions that Katie wanted to ask. On the surface it looked simple enough. Pickers working hard in the fields, the girls bunching the flowers to be driven off to this place called Mainland Marketing before being flown off to the mainland. But there was obviously much more to it than that.

'The ones the men are picking today will go in the cold store,' Becky said. 'We keep them at a temperature of one to two degrees until we despatch them to Mainland Marketing on the first stage of their journey. That won't be until tomorrow now. Visibility's bad so the planes are grounded this afternoon.'

She spoke cheerfully and yet the concern must always be there, Katie thought, because of the precariousness of the weather.

The girls drank their coffee quickly and were back at their bunching. Katie watched them, admiring the speed at which they worked.

'I expect you know that the land is owned by the Duchy of Cornwall?'

Becky said. 'We all have one-year leases for the land that are renewed each year.'

'You mean you could be given notice?'

Becky's eyes shone with amusement.

'In theory, I suppose, but highly unlikely. You'd have to do something pretty awful for that to happen. Mostly the farms remain in the same family for generations like this one. Jarrel Farm, too, of course.'

Katie was thoughtful. She had never seen Jarrel Farm as busy as it was here. In fact, she hadn't seen Mark particularly busy at all. He had complained that his cousin Rory was always breathing down his neck, but it seemed this was necessary if he was as laid-back as he seemed. She felt a spurt of sympathy for Rory.

An engine had started up now in the outer section and she heard voices. She hoped she wasn't in the way, when they were so busy.

When she mentioned this Becky laughed.

'Bob's just sending the lads to start on picking the Scilly Whites. They're early ones like the Innisidgens and the Sols.'

'Soleil d'Or,' Katie said, pleased she remembered what Mark had told her.

Becky's laugh was infectious and Katie laughed with her.

'I'm learning, you see,' she said.

'Come and see some more. Or am I boring you?'

'Of course not,' Katie said, indignant. 'It's fascinating.'

'Anyone would think it was in your blood.'

'I wish.'

'It's a hard life, you know, but we're used to it. Let me show you the boxes ready to go off when we get the call.'

They had finished their coffee now. Helen and Abby paused in their bunching as Katie waved a hand in farewell. Becky led the way into the larger room.

'The tazetas don't require a drop in

winter temperature to get going and that's why they're the early ones,' Becky said. 'That's an advantage we have over here.'

Becky's enthusiasm as she explained something of the work involved was evident. As she talked, Katie was aware of the activity around them as one of the men she had seen earlier carried in some rolls of plastic and stored them in one gloomy corner. There were boxes of narcissi in bloom in another, some white and others yellow like rays of sweetly scented sunshine in the wet afternoon.

'We can't do anything with those,' Becky said as she saw Katie looking at them. 'Too late for market. I take some down to the school and the rest get ditched. Take some with you when you go, Katie, please do.'

'Thank you.'

Becky was moving towards the boxes of flowers now and selecting some from each variety for her. She found a piece of newspaper to wrap them in.

'Not very elegant,' she said. 'Don't forget to collect them on the way out. But first let's go up to the house. We'll have another coffee there with Mum. Rory's still out there somewhere with Bob.'

'Rory Hobson?' Katie took a quick breath. She had thought him miles away and yet he was close by.

'We're thinking of converting some of the outbuildings for holiday lets. He and Bob are old friends, and Rory's doing the plans.'

Without waiting for an answer she handed Katie the cape and led the way out of the barn. The heavy rain had stopped now but thin drizzle was making the outside world seem dreary still. Water plopped from the gutter into a puddle in the doorway and there was the smell of mud and diesel oil.

Becky's husband was nowhere to be seen. Rory would be deep in concentration, too, no doubt.

The house was set back a little further from the road with a view of the bulb fields that stretched downhill in the other direction. They found Enid in the warm kitchen.

'Hello, Katie,' Enid greeted her. 'I'm glad to see you. What a day!' She glanced out at the misted-up window and gave an exaggerated sigh.

Becky had already switched on the kettle and was reaching for the coffee container.

'Bob will be bringing Rory in soon,' he said. 'Dripping wet, the pair of them, I expect, and talking of nothing but measurements and estimates and such like. The new holiday lets must be up and running by Easter. Rory's a good friend to us. He'll see to it.'

'We were surprised to see him over here on Scilly again so soon, weren't we, Becky?' Enid said.

Katie seated herself on one of the stools at the table that Becky indicated. As Becky poured the coffee, Katie couldn't help thinking that she needed to be away from here before Rory found her and complained Jane had been left alone long enough.

Enid hoisted herself up on a stool opposite and sat with both elbows on the table. She looked at Katie encouragingly.

'How is my good friend Jane?'

Katie replied to Enid's question and told her about her plans to cut a way through to Jarrel Farm so that Jane could have a level walk to see her grandson if she so wished. She hesitated, longing to confide her misgivings about Rory's cousin Mark to sympathetic listeners.

'Relax, Katie dear,' Enid said. 'Bob'll keep Rory talking out there for hours yet.'

Katie's face was warm.

'I should be on my way,' she said.

Enid smiled.

'You're not trying to avoid me, by any chance? Or are you trying to avoid someone else?'

'Mother!'

'No secrets between friends, eh, Katie?'

'Enemies if you carry on like this.' Becky shot her mother a warning glance. 'You're being embarrassing.'

Katie picked her mug and took a careful sip.

'Jane will be waking up from her afternoon rest soon.'

Enid nodded in approval.

'So nice to have someone with your interests at heart.'

She ducked to one side in exaggerated fear as her daughter picked up the milk jug and brandished it at her.

Katie laughed, loving the banter between them. She was still smiling when she was on her way home clutching an armful of narcissi.

The clouds were clearing to a fine afternoon, the woody scent from the banks was enchanting and there was still no sign of Rory.

13

Caught in the Act

For some reason Katie felt restless on her return from Liberty Farm. Perhaps it was because life was easy here at the cottage in contrast to Becky's busy one. Katie moved a chair nearer the table in the sitting-room and straightened the cloth Jane liked to have on it.

The scent from some of Liberty Farm's narcissi was almost overpowering in this small space but Jane was delighted with them and wanted them near her. Katie paused for a moment and then moved the chair back to its original position.

Jane looked at her over the top of her glasses.

'Another walk perhaps? There's plenty of time before tea.'

'A walk? Well, yes, that would be

good. Will you come, too?'

'Not today, dear. Another time, perhaps. Off you go then, and get rid of some of that pent-up energy.'

Katie smiled. Something was driving her, something that wouldn't let her mind rest, and Jane understood her need for action.

Moments later her jacket was on and she was pulling on her hiking boots. And now here she was with the shears in her hand, making her way to the start of what she intended to be the way through to Jarrel Farm after years of neglect.

She stopped in surprise. Someone had been here before her, using something far more powerful than a pair of shears. With the brambles gone and stacked against walls that until now had been almost invisible the path looked wider and more like the track of long ago that Jane had described. There was a strong scent of cut grass and foliage.

Katie gazed at it in wonder.

Mark had talked of a scythe. Now it looked as if he had done something positive about using it. Well done, Mark! She had misjudged him.

Stepping carefully, Katie moved along the ground that was bumpy and uneven in places and would need constant use to flatten the surface. Her pace quickened.

Somewhere above her a lone seagull glided in the fresh air, uttering a bleak call. Every day she would make a point of walking along here and others might too, now that they could see that there was an obvious way through to the coastal path.

Thanks to Mark, she reached the outbuildings of Jarrel Farm much sooner than she expected. The two holiday apartments built on to the rear of the farmhouse looked charming from this side in the late afternoon sunlight, but as she got nearer she saw the long unkempt grass between them and the boundary wall and the piles of rubbish stacked nearby.

Perhaps now Mark would do something about all that. But it was not yet December and months away from the start of the holiday season. There was plenty of time to sort that lot out.

Becky Tait had been excited about their plans for converting some of their own outbuildings in time for the first visitors and they hadn't even been started yet.

'There is always room for more holiday accommodation,' she had said, her eyes alight with enthusiasm. 'We will make sure that they reach the highest quality. Rory's the man for that. He's had some brilliant ideas.'

Like the other flower farmers, Mark needed to diversify and Katie hoped he would make a success of it for the good name of the Hobson family. So how would they compare with the Taits' new properties?

On a sudden impulse, Katie placed the shears at the edge of the path and clambered over the low disintegrating wall. She tramped through the wet grass, determined to check for herself. She hoped that Mark's conversion wasn't as bad as she had thought when he showed her round the other day but she feared very much that it was. There was only one way to check.

The smeary windows of the first apartment were difficult to peer through but she could see enough to distinguish the red walls of the kitchen. It was little more than a passageway with few units and only a small working surface. Surely self-catering properties should have a decent space for the preparation of food?

She looked through the window of the next one and found it just the same, with one huge difference. There were patches of damp on the opposite wall. She looked more closely. Water was trickling down it from the ceiling to the floor.

Katie tried the door handle, found it unlocked, and went inside. She expected the place to smell damp but there was a musty smell, too, from the matting underfoot.

She slipped her boots off and went to check the bathroom, turning on both taps to see if they were working. They were. She turned them off again with an extra hard twist.

Nothing wrong in here that she could see or in the bedrooms, each equipped with a bed, bare of bedding, which took up virtually all the space.

Moments later she was padding across the kitchen floor to slip her boots back on. She needed to notify Mark at once.

★ ★ ★

Rory Hobson spread his plans out on his kitchen table and pulled it nearer the window for maximum light. His brief at Liberty Farm had been much as he expected and a pleasure to sort out. Bob had taken most of his ideas on board and had been grateful for his input.

'I couldn't have found a better man,' he had said, slapping Rory on the back. 'A bit of luck you were over here at this time.'

Luck? That was one way of putting it, Rory supposed. It had been luck in a way that the St Martin's project was ongoing and he'd been able to get away from his office to attend to it.

Doing so was becoming easier as time went on because he was gradually sorting out his professional life to be able to work more and more from home. And home, now, was definitely the Isles of Scilly.

So he had smiled and agreed.

He had known the Taits for years. He and Bob had been at school here together on St Mary's and had both chosen the same sixth-form college on the mainland before going on to further education, he to De Montfort University in Leicester to study architecture, and Bob to agricultural college in the Cotswolds.

There Bob had met Becky, and

within a year or two had married her and brought her back to the Isles of Scilly. This had pleased her family who had lived here for at least two generations.

Becky always said that her escape from the islands hadn't worked out so she had snapped Bob up so as to return without loss of face. No-one, seeing them together, believed them, of course.

It was a pity that Becky hadn't been around this afternoon but she was busy in the bunching shed, entertaining someone who wanted to learn about the flower industry. He was surprised to hear that it was Katie. And secretly pleased.

There was a hint of repressed energy about her that needed more of an outlet than looking after an old lady who was determined to be independent. An interest in life around her could only be good.

'Rory?'

Rory gave a start.

'Yes, Bob, I'm with you.'

'Wishing you were out of here and back on the mainland?'

He grinned. Bob knew him too well to think that.

'Right, then,' he said, focusing on the matter in hand. 'Let's get on with it. That French door you wanted from the kitchen area to the patio . . . '

He must have done a good job because Bob was clearly satisfied. The location was ideal with plenty of room behind each of the proposed properties for a paved area and lawn. And the view across the sloping bulb fields to the sea would delight any holidaymaker's heart.

Becky was in the house with her mother when he and Bob got there at last for a warm-up and a welcome cup of coffee. Rory had thought that Katie might have been here, too, but obviously she thought she shouldn't leave his grandmother long on her own, though she was entitled to free time each day.

He should have been pleased instead of disappointed but somehow her sense of duty irked him a little.

'Something wrong?' Becky asked.

'Very much all right,' he said, warming himself at the Aga.

'Then come and sit down,' Enid said, her voice crisp. She shot him a knowing look. 'No need standing there looking as if you've lost a valuable coin and found a penny.'

Now, back in his own cottage at Porthcressa, he wondered exactly what Enid had been getting at. He sighed and then remembered that he needed to firm up a few details and add them to the plans he had already prepared on computer.

Then he would visit Jarrel Farm to run an eye over the place in Mark's absence as he had promised.

*　*　*

Katie had trouble pulling the door shut behind her. Damp must have swelled

154

the wood. Another thing to be looked at.

She leaned against it for a moment it to regain her breath and saw a figure approaching from the side of the first apartment. He was carrying her shears.

'These must be yours.'

A giggle rose in her throat and was swiftly swallowed back. Rory was looking at her with a questioning look and the expression in his eyes looked serious. Surely he didn't regard them as an offensive weapon?

'Do many people leave shears lying about on the path?' she said.

'Only when they don't need to use them.'

She put out her hand for them and then drew it back. A pair of shears wasn't the issue here. Visiting the new holiday apartments uninvited was, especially as she had been inside one of them.

She owed him an explanation.

'I needed to check on something,' she said, her voice expressionless. 'The door

was unlocked. There's a leak somewhere. I have to tell Mark.'

'Mark's not here. He's on the
mainland for three days.'

'Oh.'

'You didn't know?'

She shook her head. The implication
here was that she had waited until he
was gone before she came snooping
round.

'I was passing, that's all.'

'And you assumed something needed
checking?'

'No, I . . . '

She broke off in dismay. There was
something odd here.

'Wait a minute. How did you know I
didn't need the shears?'

'I thought you had walked over from
the cottage.'

'And you were sure I could get
through now, when it's been completely
overgrown for years.'

'That's about it. This leak, then. I'd
better take a look.'

She followed him inside.

156

'You checked the other rooms?' he said.

She nodded.

He kneeled down and pulled open the cupboard door beneath the sink. He reached in and gave a grunt of satisfaction.

On his feet again, he said nothing. The dripping had stopped once the stopcock had been switched off — she hadn't thought to do that herself. Another black mark against her, and one she deserved. She bit her lip and wished she were a million miles away.

He gave her a look but the condemnation she expected to see wasn't there.

'This is Mark's problem,' he said. 'He'll be back tomorrow and can sort out the plumber then.'

He held the door open for her and followed her outside. She was glad of the breeze to cool her hot cheeks.

'Are you heading back now?' he said. 'I can give you a lift if you like.'

She needed space and distance.

Averting her face, she picked up the shears and shook her head.

'I'll walk back, thanks.' Her resolve to keep away from him was hard enough as it was without being in the confined space of his car, close to him.

'Give my love to my grandmother.'

'I will.' She escaped through the long clinging grass.

The quickest way to the path was the way she had come over the wall. She didn't wait to see his reaction to that. He hadn't asked her reason for looking closely at the holiday lets and she wasn't going to tell him.

She was halfway along the path when a thought struck her. Mark hadn't been on Scilly for the last few days, so he couldn't have scythed a way along the path. So it must have been Rory who had set to work.

It was obvious, now she thought about it. He was a busy man over here only on short visits but he had done this!

For one moment she felt uplifted but

that was quickly dashed. It might have been on Mark's agenda anyway, to give his holiday visitors a shortcut to the coast, and he had mentioned it to Rory who thought it a good and practical idea.

Her help with the picking was obviously on Rory's mind if Mark needed it so badly, and clearing the path would make it easier for her to get between the two dwellings.

Jarrel Farm was the important thing here and the need for it to thrive would be uppermost in Rory's mind.

14

A Place in Her Heart

Flushed with success, Enid greeted Katie with warmth on Saturday afternoon. The craft fair was heaving and Katie wondered where all the people had come from.

She viewed Enid's empty stall with dismay.

'I'm too late, aren't I?'

'You couldn't persuade Jane to come with you?'

Katie smiled and shrugged. Enid knew the answer to that already but she wasn't one to give up.

'That's why I couldn't be here this morning. She was so distressed when I mentioned it that I felt I must stay with her. It looks as if you did really well.'

'So well that I can pack up now.' Enid's self-satisfaction made Katie smile. 'Take a look round while I see to it, there's a dear, and then we can go for cup of tea, or mulled wine, perhaps. Such an enticing smell. Becky's here somewhere about, just like everyone else.'

Except Rory, Katie thought. She had already caught sight of Mark with a dark-haired girl. They were buying an artificial arrangement of what looked like dried seaweed, feathers and white pebbles.

Other stalls were doing a brisk trade in Christmas decorations. There was a tree in the corner shining with flickering red lights.

The evocative scent of pine needles and spice and her sudden spurt of happiness took Katie by surprise. It was all so happy and innocent and she was part of it, caught up in the excitement and good humour.

Last Christmas she had been with Dad in their Truro home. Although the sadness was still with her, the atmosphere here was heartening. She had come for Jane's sake, to be able to tell her just how it was and how her friend Enid was doing at something she loved. Now she was pleased to be here for her own enjoyment.

She bought a jar of homemade lemon curd and another of mincemeat. Then she saw some hand-decorated note-books, each covered in material of different colours and patterns. She exclaimed in pleasure and picked one up with a design in creams and yellows that made her think of how the bulb fields would be if left on their own to burst into glorious bloom.

The softness of the cover felt wonderful. Jane would love it.

'I'd like this one, please.' She looked at the person behind the stall and saw that it was Glenda. 'Oh! I didn't see you.'

'Yes, it's me.' Glenda's smile lit up her face. 'So flattering that you were concentrating on my poor efforts.'

'Did you do all these?'

'One of my hidden talents.'

'You have hidden ones as well? I'm impressed. This one's for Jane. She'll be so interested.'

So would a few other people she knew. Anna would love that bigger one in muted shades of pink and purple. She bought three more, one of them for herself.

Now Enid was ready to carry her off for some refreshment.

'I need to speak to Harold, the treasurer, on the way through,' she said. 'It won't take a minute. You go ahead and choose a table, Katie. It's through there.'

It was more a question of finding a free table, Katie saw as she entered the large conservatory away from the main room. She stood, irresolute, and then headed for a small one across the room where two people were preparing to go.

She was lucky to find somewhere so quickly but dare not move across to join the queue for refreshment or she would be in danger of losing it. Enid's idea of not being long was way off the mark.

'May I?'

Katie, startled, looked up to see Rory standing close by, holding a laden tray. Without waiting for permission he placed the tray on the table and sat down in the only available chair.

'Sorry, Enid's sitting there.'

He made an exaggerated movement to indicate surprise.

'Beneath me, you mean?'

'She'd be squashed flat if she were.'

Rory grinned.

'She sent me instead of her so there's no need to worry. Insisted on it, in fact, and she's not a lady to cross. So, here I am with a jug of mulled wine, enough for two. I hope you like these mince puff things. They look mouth-watering, don't you think? Enid's choice, of course.'

'Of course,' Katie said, smiling.

'You're laughing at me. You think I'm a weak reed unable to stand up to a woman, small though she is. The truth is, I need to talk to you away from Jarrel Cottage, and this is a good opportunity.'

'So it's not entirely the lure of my personality that brought you here?'

He lifted everything from the tray on to the table and handed Katie a plate and a knife. Then, very carefully, he poured from the jug into the glasses.

All around them the sounds were muted now and it seemed to Katie that they were the only people in this fine conservatory with its high glass ceiling and feeling of light and space.

The mince puff, when she bit into it, was as delicious as it looked.

Suddenly he smiled.

'You're wondering why I'm here.'

He was easily the most handsome man in the room, she thought, and one who made her insides sing if she allowed herself to admit her true feelings.

But that was impossible. Her stomach was churning in a ridiculous way because of his hidden agenda which he seemed curiously reluctant to divulge. She could only think the worst, that he was giving her notice because the few weeks of her contract were nearing an end. He had made no secret of the fact that he considered her too inexperienced for the job.

She took a sip of her mulled wine and her hand shook as she put down the glass. He had no right to spoil a happy afternoon like this with serious talk about something he might know would bring distress.

She gathered up her bag.

'I've no need to wonder,' she said. 'I think I can guess what it's all about.'

'You can?'

She looked at him in surprise at the lightness of his tone. In fact, now she came to think of it, he was looking at her in a friendly way.

'I've a boat arranged for a visit to St Martin's on Monday,' he said. 'I was hoping you'd agree to accompany me.'

She felt the colour leave her face and then flood back again.

'You want me to go with you? But why?'

His lips twitched.

'I'd better not say that Enid thought it a good idea.'

'Enid again!'

'She seems to be on your case, Katie. But I have to say that she has a point. You need some time off away from my grandmother and this would be a good way to provide it.

'I have to go over there to consult with a client and it's an opportunity for you to visit another island. No problem in the summer, of course, with the boats going out every day, but another matter out of season. What do you say?'

She hardly knew what to say. One minute he was implying that she shouldn't leave his grandmother too long on her own and the next he was suggesting a day away from St Mary's. Added to that was her resolve to keep out of his company whenever possible. Of course she shouldn't go with him.

'How long would it take?' she said.

'The afternoon, that's all. We'll be over there for about an hour, not long. It'll give you a taste of what it's like and you might enjoy the boat trip. In case you're wondering, Enid plans to visit Gram.'

She smiled and his answering one held a hint of mischief. It was a lovely moment full of what might have been.

Pink jacket, she reminded herself. This was a friendly gesture only.

'Of course I'll come.'

He nodded.

'I'll pick you up about one-thirty. Weather permitting, of course.'

Yes, the weather, she thought, immediately dashed. The weather that ruled their lives. But if they couldn't go this time there might well be another chance, a little secret voice told her. The thought was uplifting.

★　★　★

The quay was deserted this grey Monday afternoon and strangely quiet. There was not even a muted cry from the gulls swooping in the sky above them. The water in the harbour was steely grey but out beyond a few moored boats Katie could see rough sea rippling with the dark shadow of wind.

She made sure that her jacket was zipped up as far as it would go. Rory, though, seemed impervious to cold. His jacket was half-open and the jersey beneath it only a light one.

He was laden down with a laptop and a large cardboard folder that looked awkward to carry.

He gave her an encouraging smile as they stood together in the shelter of the office building.

'Derek will be here soon,' he said. 'Hear that chugging noise? That'll be him now. His boat's smaller than the usual summer boats that take the visitors to the off-islands,' he said. 'But there's a small cabin if you're cold.'

With Derek the boatman's help, Katie stepped aboard and sat on one of the outside seats so she could look over the side. Rory seated himself beside her, placing his laptop and folder at his feet. Derek cast off and they were away.

The noise from the engine should have drowned out any chance of conversation between him and Rory but Derek didn't let that deter him. He had such a booming voice for a small man and questioned Rory vigorously about building plans until they had left the harbour behind them. He then lapsed in silence.

The sea was rougher now and Katie enjoyed the movement, though the odd splash of water on her face took her by surprise. Laughing, she turned to Rory.

'This is the life!'

His answering smile indicated that he felt the same.

Hugh Town was well behind them now and she tried to pick out some of the landmarks on St Mary's as they hugged the coastline for a while before heading out across the sea. It all looked so different from here, she thought. For some time St Martin's seemed no nearer than when she had looked across at its golden beaches from the coastal path near the cottage although they were moving fast.

And then they were almost there. She knew from the map that St Martin's was the second-largest of the islands and that its beaches were some of the finest.

The engine noise dwindled to a quiet hum as Derek brought the boat close to the quay. There was a truck parked nearby, obviously waiting for Rory.

'Would you like to come, too, Katie,' he asked, 'or would you rather explore on your own?'

She hesitated. An hour, Rory had told her, and most of that time he would be involved with his client and she would be in the way. An hour wasn't long but she would like to see something of the island.

'I'll meet you back here, shall I?'

He nodded.

The beach she had seen from the coast path near the cottage was close by and looked irresistible. She set off along it, picturing in her mind how it would be in high summer with families

171

enjoying themselves in the clear water and picnicking on this lovely stretch of sand.

The grassy area above the beach would be full of the huge blue agapanthus she had seen in photographs of Scilly and longed to see for herself. But she would be long gone by then, intent on pursuing whatever career she had decided on during these four weeks she was here.

And there was the rub. She hadn't given a thought to her future and only now did it occur to her that she needed to contact her solicitor to check the position with Dad's house, and whether or not she was at liberty to go ahead with the sale.

Then what? The thought of leaving the islands was painful. Life here was so different, so away from it all, so innocent somehow.

Perhaps the quality of the air had something to do with it, she thought, and then laughed at being so over-imaginative.

They were in December now with Christmas not far away, yet there was none of the pre-Christmas frenzy. She liked that. Yes, life was hard, she had seen that for herself. But she knew, wherever she was, that these islands out in the Atlantic would always hold a special place in her heart.

She wasn't going to let thoughts about that cloud this lovely moment. She walked on to the end of the beach and then reluctantly turned back. As she did so the sun burst through the remaining clouds and bathed the beach in golden light.

★ ★ ★

As she approached the quay and found Rory waiting for her, Katie could see that he was pleased with his afternoon's work. He had chosen a place to sit in a sheltered position on some weathered planks of wood. He looked at peace with the world. She sat down beside him.

'How did your afternoon go?' she said.

'There's nothing like being on the spot to sort out any problems,' he said. 'The client's happy now and so am I. Not only that, but I've gained another commission, a smaller project but welcome all the same.'

'So it was worthwhile coming?'

He smiled.

'It was definitely that.'

There was something in the way he was looking at her that seemed to indicate more than mere professional pleasure at being here on St Martin's.

As they waited for Derek to come back after visiting some of his St Martin's family, Rory told her more of what his work entailed and she realised she was getting to know the man better, too, and to understand a little of what made him the way he was. He didn't say so but she also gathered, by a few brief allusions to the Hobson flower farm, of how much that place meant to him.

They voyaged home to St Mary's through a calmer sea now. Sitting next to Rory in the stern, Katie felt relaxed and content with the world. She thought of Anna back there in Truro and of the life she lived among her family, with plenty going on around her, while she, Katie, was working for just a few hours in a place most people would think of as isolated. And yet this felt right for the moment.

And for longer? This was something she hadn't dared think about.

'You look thoughtful,' Rory said. 'Are you wishing you were back on the mainland among people you've known for years?'

She smiled.

'I was born and grew up in Falmouth and it still seems like home, although Dad and I moved to Truro after my mother died when I was sixteen.'

'You've no brothers or sisters?'

'No. I've some good friends, though. Anna took me under her wing from the first and we've been close friends ever since. It was Anna who egged me on to answer your advertisement.'

'And do you regret it?'

She looked at him solemnly.

'Not so far.'

He laughed.

'My grandmother doesn't, either. She feels you're an ally. But those stairs in the cottage are not good. She needs somewhere all on one level, but won't hear of any change.'

'I was wondering if we couldn't bring a bed downstairs,' Katie said. 'The sitting-room would make a good bedroom for her and there's plenty of room in the kitchen for some easy chairs. It's sunnier, too, all day, with easier access to the garden.'

'You've been thinking it all out.'

'Yes, but I haven't dared mention it.'

'Wise girl.'

'A coward.'

He looked at her fondly.

'Never that.'

The drive from the quay to Jarrel Cottage was all too swift and in no time at all, it seemed, Katie was greeting Enid and Jane and explaining that Rory had some important work to do and would call in tomorrow if he had time.

'That's a busy architect for you,' Enid said and she prepared to depart.

Jane smiled.

'He's very good to me.'

Katie closed the door behind Jane's friend at last and saw the pink jacket hanging on the hook behind it, unnoticed by any of them until now.

She stared at it.

'But that's . . . '

'Enid up to her tricks again,' Jane said with a sigh, 'leaving her belongings all over the place. She's only just got that particular jacket back from Rory. She'll leave her head behind one of these days!'

Katie laughed rather shakily.

But later, as she got ready for bed, her heart sang and she fell asleep remembering Rory's every word and every look as they waited together on St Martin's for the home crossing.

15

Accident at the Cottage

Next day the phone rang at breakfast time. Katie got up to answer it and on her return to the kitchen she smiled at Jane, hoping she would be pleased that Mark had contacted them after days of silence.

'Good news, dear?'

'The best. That was Mark. He sends his love.'

'And?' Jane was not to be fooled. She was only too aware that he didn't often phone without some good reason.

Katie sat down and continued spreading marmalade on her cooling toast.

'He needs a picker. He's asked me to do some this afternoon if it's OK with you.'

Jane frowned.

'On a Sunday afternoon? That would never have been allowed in the old days. So his usual one is unable to do it?'

'Something like that. He sounded desperate and I'd like to help.'

'Then he must pay you the usual rate.'

'I'm a learner, don't forget, and it's only for a couple of hours.'

'Even so.'

Katie could tell that Jane would have said more but decided against it and so didn't pursue it herself. Payment wasn't on her mind, anyway. She had wanted an insight into an important part of Scilly life and this was a good way to get it.

She wore her oldest clothes and set off along the newly-cut footpath that afternoon at a brisk pace. The tractor with the cart attached stood in the yard. In it were several empty plastic containers.

'Jump on,' Mark said when he saw her.

Riding behind him on the tractor, Katie felt part of the scene even before they arrived at the field a short distance away.

'We need five hundred stems plus,' he told her as they jumped down. 'I'll start you off and then get back later to pick you up.'

Katie began with the row at the edge of the field, picking each stem as Mark had shown her. She didn't see him leave and was only aware that she was alone when she straightened and looked round.

She had been counting as she picked. Forty stems, that was all, and time was passing. It was as many as she could hold in one go and she walked back to the cart and placed them upright in one of the containers, as Mark said he wanted them. She was pleased to see that there were at least as many as that in the container already.

She had thought the wind was chilly when she started but as she speeded up on the job she felt the trickle of sweat down her back that was aching now.

She rested for a few moments and then started off again, determined not to give in. On she went, returning to the cart each time she had picked forty stems.

At last, she heard Mark's voice and picked a few more quickly before joining him.

'How're you doing?'

Her face was burning and she could hardly stand upright.

'I reckon I've almost got there.'

He examined the container.

'That'll do, I reckon. Come on, jump on.'

She had been too tired to glance at her watch before but now she saw that the two hours hadn't passed yet, although it had seemed much longer. Her respect for the pickers who did this day in day out in all weathers increased a hundredfold.

Back at the farm, Mark lifted out the container and carried it into an inner room where Katie hadn't been before.

It was much like the one at Liberty Farm but much untidier and the floor was covered with a carpet of dust and wood shavings that stuck to Katie's damp trainers.

'Like to do a bit of bunching next time?'

'Why not?' It must be easier than the picking and she would be sitting down.

'Come back tomorrow morning, then,' he said in an offhand manner, 'as early as you like. These will go in the cold store now, ready to be go off after that. The bunching can wait.'

'Oh.' She was disappointed. Mark must have known that the afternoon was her official time off or had forgotten.

At that moment a car pulled up outside and she heard a door slam. Katie's heart raced to see Rory striding across the yard. He stopped short on seeing her.

'I've been helping Mark,' she said. 'He needed a picker.'

Rory swung round to face his cousin.

'You've had another order?'

'If it's any business of yours,' Mark said.

'Katie is my business. She's in my employ and I won't let her be put upon.'

'That's enough!' Katie cried. Both men stared at her as if they had forgotten she was actually present. 'Mark asked me if I wanted to do it and I agreed,' she said, 'This is my free time in the afternoons. You can't object to that.'

'Afternoons?' Mark said, dismayed. 'So you'll need to get them bunched now, then?'

'I hope you're paying her the going rate?' Rory's voice was accusing. 'I thought as much.'

Katie was aware of Rory standing there watching their every move as Mark, ignoring him, indicated a place for her to sit at the bench. She saw that a container of elastic bands stood at one side. Her hands trembled a little as she began.

Mark said nothing but she could feel the animosity between them and was relieved when the two of them left her to it. She had to stop every now and again to wipe the slimy sap from her fingers but at last she was finished.

Mark came back into the room looking pleased with himself. Rory had obviously driven off.

She stood up and stretched.

'I've learned a lot,' she said, 'and I've been glad to help out this afternoon.'

'So you'll come again?'

She smiled, weary though she was.

'Of course I will, any time.'

She dragged herself home. The path that had seemed so short on her way here now appeared to be unending.

Before she left she had watched Mark open the door into the cold room to place the container inside. At Liberty Farm their cold room had been lined with shelves and the floor was clean and uncluttered.

Comparing them wasn't really fair but her impression of this one was that it hardly knew what it was meant for.

In fact, now she came to think of it, it hadn't felt any colder than the room in which she had spent time bunching the narcissi. Jane would be concerned if she thought Mark wasn't prospering here at Jarrel Farm, and worry wasn't good for her.

★ ★ ★

The cottage, when she arrived, seemed unusually quiet. The sitting-room fire must have gone out because no smoke was rising from the chimney. Anxious for no good reason except that it was getting late, Katie hurried round to the back so she could leave her trainers as usual by the back door.

The kitchen was just as she had left it with the washed lunch dishes still on the draining board waiting to be put away when she got back. In passing she felt the kettle. It was cold.

She opened the door into the hall. There, on the floor at the foot of the stairs, lay Jane. Katie ran forward and kneeled at her side to feel for her pulse. As she did so, Jane stirred.

'Katie?' she murmured.

She was already struggling to sit up but gave up and lay down again, her face white.

'I fell. My ankle . . . '

'It could be broken,' Katie said, her heart thudding. 'We'll need help.' She was on her feet now, reaching for the phone.

'The ambulance will be here soon. Keep still, Jane, please. I'll get a cushion, your blanket . . . '

Katie was back at once, kneeling down again to manoeuvre the cushion beneath Jane's head and to cover her with the blanket. Her hands were cold.

'I fell.' Jane's voice was weak. 'It's nothing. I . . . '

'I'm here now,' Katie said. 'I'll look after you.'

'You're a good girl, Katie.'

But not good enough, Katie thought. She was back later than she had intended and that definitely was bad.

But there wasn't time to dwell on that before she heard a vehicle pull up outside. She leaped up to open the front door.

'Thank goodness you're here.'

Katie stood back as the men questioned Jane and with great care examined her ankle. At last one nodded to the other. A fold-up stretcher was brought and Jane was lifted on to it.

16

A Friend in Need

At any other time Katie would have appreciated the view from the hospital on the hill above Porthcressa. Today she thought only of staying close to Jane for as long as possible.

Jane had said nothing as they drove in the ambulance down to Hugh Town but Katie was aware that she was glad of her presence by the way she gripped her hand.

When Jane was carried off, leaving Katie to wait on her own, she sat down on a chair opposite the door.

Time passed. She thought of Mark back there at the farm, and of Rory. Of course she must phone him. She should have done that at once.

She checked for a signal and walked across to the window. He was home and told her he would come immediately.

The last time she had seen him he had been annoyed with Mark and their argument had sounded fierce. Now, when he came through the door into the waiting-room, he looked so solid and dependable that she felt tears spring to her eyes. She wanted to fling herself against his chest and feel his strong arms round her.

She took a deep breath and swallowed hard. She looked up at Rory and saw the sympathy in his slight smile as sat down beside her. He was quick to go straight to the heart of things.

'Any news?'

She shook her head.

'Tell me what happened.'

She did so and he listened carefully without commenting. She wondered why he didn't contact Mark. Could it be that he was afraid his cousin would breeze in, full of suggestions about Jane's future that didn't tally with his own?

And what of her own position?

Ashamed of the selfishness of that thought, she banished it immediately.

'I'll make some enquiries,' Rory said.

Before he left the room he walked across to the drinks machine and returned to her with two steaming paper mugs.

'Here, drink that.'

She took it gratefully and held her hands round it until it was cool enough to drink.

* * *

They stood looking down over Hugh Town from the top of the steep footpath that led down to Rory's cottage. The view was breathtaking and one that Katie hadn't seen before. There were the grey buildings of the small town with Porthcressa beach on one side and the town beach on the other. Two sea views at once, she thought.

The air on Katie's face felt fresh and exhilarating. Day in, day out, this view was here and she hadn't known it. With

Rory beside her everything seemed well, even the knowledge that Jane must remain in hospital while her ankle was being set and tests done of her general health.

At last Rory stirred and she saw that the lines round his eyes had deepened.

'Exhausted?' he asked.

She nodded.

'You, too?'

'We need to eat. My cottage or better still, the nearest pub. A good idea?'

'Perfect.'

They found a table near the window.

'Fish and chips?' he suggested. 'For quickness.'

She smiled her agreement. It looked delicious when it came and seemed to her the best she had ever tasted.

Rory agreed.

'It's the shock kicking in. We need it.'

Katie's cheeks felt flushed with warmth and she found the cheerful noise around them comforting. She wanted to sit here for a long time instead of returning to a cold and empty cottage.

When her dad died his flat had been unbearable. This time, though, she knew that Jane would recover and it wasn't the end of everything for her. But would her grandsons allow her to return?

She glanced at Rory and could see nothing but concern in his face.

He seemed as reluctant as she was to leave this lively place full of warmth and good humour, but more people were crowding in now looking for somewhere to sit. Outside, the rising wind sent flurries of white-capped wavelets across the water in the harbour and there was the threat of rain in the lowering sky.

Rory looked even more weary but before he could say anything she whipped out her phone and clicked on Handy Taxis' number. No way would she give Rory the chance to offer her a lift home. For one thing, the walk back to his place to collect his car seemed more than she could manage, short though it was.

'My taxi will be here soon,' she said.

Rory seemed about to say something but then changed his mind. She didn't look round as the taxi set off but settled back in her seat, remembering the first time she had ridden in this same car when she had first arrived on Scilly. Then she had been apprehensive about her welcome at Jarrel Cottage. Now she felt so much for the place that the thought of leaving it was distressing.

*   *   *

To her surprise, Katie slept well that night, worn out, no doubt, by guilt because she wasn't here at the time of Jane's accident. But it had happened and there was nothing now that she could do about it except phone the hospital for visiting times.

It was doubtful whether they would tell her how Jane was getting on as she wasn't next of kin. Also, she must phone Liberty Farm to tell Becky and her mother what had happened. Neither of the calls took long.

The cottage was as quiet as it always was but now there was an added deepness to the silence because its owner wasn't here. Katie picked up the phone again and dialled Anna's number.

Anna answered at once.

'Oh, Anna, it's good to hear your voice,' Katie said, a lump in her throat.

'Katie. How are things with you over there on that tropical island?'

Katie gave a shaky laugh.

'Something's happened, Anna. Jane had an accident. She fell down the stairs. She's in hospital.'

There was a second's horrified silence and then Anna spoke.

'And you're blaming yourself?'

Katie poured it all out, knowing it was the best thing she could do and Anna would at once be sympathetic and bracing at the same time.

'So when did it happen?' she said.

'Sometime during the afternoon. I don't know exactly when, and that's the awful part, Anna. I should have been here.'

'You said she fell down the stairs?'

'It's a difficult staircase and very narrow.'

'So she can't have fallen far.'

'Well, no.'

'And how would you have stopped her if you'd been there?'

There was that, of course. Katie moved a little in her chair. She would have heard it happen, though, and been on the spot to do something at once.

'So what happened to that contract of yours, Katie? Three hours of light housework, wasn't it, if I remember rightly, in exchange for board and lodging? I can't remember anything about being responsible for your hostess twenty-four-seven. Did I miss something?'

'No, but . . . '

'Sounds as clear as glass to me.'

'Oh, Anna.'

Her friend's voice softened.

'I know, I know. You've grown fond of Jane and she of you and you feel totally responsible for her. It's just the way you are — you need someone to care for. I wish I could be there for you. All I can do is sympathise from a distance and look forward to seeing you at Christmas. And now things might well be different for you and, of course, for Jane, too.'

'You see, this would be a perfect excuse for her grandsons making other arrangements for her, but I know how much she'll hate it. I'm so afraid they'll force her into it.'

'What can you do about that?'

Nothing, Katie knew. She felt a failure in this as well as in everything else.

'If you have to leave, Katie, remember you can come here earlier than you intended. You're always welcome.'

Katie blinked back her tears and took a deep breath.

'I know how much I can count on you, Anna, and I'm grateful.'

'You'll have me in tears in a minute.'

Katie's laugh sounded a little weak but on the other end of the phone she heard a small giggle.

She imagined how it would be if the conditions were reversed and it was she in hospital about to have her future taken over by somebody else, however well-meaning. She would fight it with all her worth.

And so would Jane. All at once her anxiety lifted a little. It would do Jane no good to know Katie was moping at home, prepared to give up.

'You're good for me, Anna,' she said.

'If you say so. What are you going to do now?'

'A shower first,' Katie said, her voice firm. 'Then bed. And in the morning I'll start on some spring-cleaning. A little early, I know. But things are different here on Scilly, tropical or not.'

'It certainly sounds like it. Go to it, girl. I shall expect a full report tomorrow evening. And the best of luck.'

Determination was what was needed here, Katie thought, as she put down the phone.

She squared her shoulders, her moment of weakness over.

Katie Robertson was on the war path and let no-one get on her way!

17

An Unexpected Kiss

Monday was a glorious day, all sunshine and glitter. It had rained in the night and now everything was drying out. She heard the first plane take off soon after nine. She wondered how soon Mark would be delivering the narcissi to Mainland Marketing on the first stage of their journey to the mainland.

By lunchtime the cottage was spotless and Katie allowed herself a brief respite to wander outside for a breath of air that felt more like March than December.

Up here at Jarrel Cottage it was hard to believe that Christmas would soon be here, or that her future now was even more uncertain.

But on a day such as this she felt her

spirits rise. Jane was being looked after and this afternoon she would cycle down to see her.

She took her lunch of sandwiches and yoghurt outside and ate it sitting on a part of the wall at the front of the cottage where someone had removed some of the stones to make a handy seat.

This was a part of the property that was warmed by any available winter sunshine and she was going to make the most of it. She had brought out a mug of coffee, too, and set it down beside her.

Not for the first time, she viewed the front of the cottage with pleasure, admiring the way yellow lichen clung to the tiled roof. The downstairs windows on either side of the door shone with her cleaning efforts. How sad Jane would be to leave it, and after her accident this seemed more likely than ever. Even now her grandsons might be plotting something.

Soon she, Katie, would be told that

her services would no longer be required and she must face that and make arrangements to leave the islands. There was nowhere she could afford to live here at the moment, even if she found work in the bulb fields or, better still, in the bunching sheds.

A few weeks ago she had never heard of Jane and her grandsons, or ever dreamed that she would find a temporary home on Scilly that would come to mean so much to her. It was strange how things worked out. And now she was on the verge of leaving it.

★ ★ ★

Jane was sitting on a chair with her foot encased in plaster propped up on a footstool. She was wearing a hospital gown with a blue shawl draped round her shoulders and looked somehow diminished without her glasses.

For a moment Katie didn't recognise her and stood irresolute.

'Katie!' Jane's eyes brightened as she

saw Katie who came nearer at once, smiling, and showed her the bag of necessities she had brought with her.

'Thank you, dear.'

'There should be everything there that you need.'

Jane wanted the curtains drawn round the cubicle immediately but refused all offers of help to change into her own nightdress.

By the time Katie had located a chair and brought it forward Jane was ready for her to pull the curtains back and to place the rest of her things in the bedside locker.

Katie handed over her glasses which had been placed safely nearby and Jane put them on.

'There,' she said in satisfaction. 'Now we're ready to talk.'

Jane looked a different person from the one Katie had first seen huddled in her chair. Relieved, she answered Jane's questions about the cottage and then asked other, more important ones, of her own even though Jane couldn't tell her much more than she already knew.

They made no mention of what would happen when Jane was eventually discharged.

Jane was looking positively animated now as if they were meeting in a happy social occasion.

Katie looked up and saw Rory approaching, ushered in by a discreet nurse who then vanished about her own business.

'Gram?'

He removed his thick jacket and bent to kiss his grandmother. He had brought with him a hint of wintry air that seemed to linger in the room.

He looked serious.

At once Katie made a movement to go but sat down again at a gesture from Rory.

'We need to talk, Gram and I,' he said, 'but not just yet. I've arranged to have a word with the doctor in about ten minutes.'

He smiled at them both and Katie

could see the sadness in his eyes and the lines deepening round his eyes. That he was under a great deal of strain was obvious and she felt a deep sadness for him.

As far as she could tell, Jane was not aware of it unless, of course, she was keeping her own counsel.

They talked of the hospital food and Rory's ability to cook delicious meals for himself when he had the opportunity.

'I hope you're finding time enough for that,' Jane said, looking at him over the top of her glasses. 'It doesn't do to neglect yourself.'

'You think I'm doing that?'

'Just look at you, sitting there as if you've lost a shilling and found sixpence.'

'I haven't heard that expression for years.'

'And I hope I don't have to use it again.'

While Rory was away, Jane entertained Katie with snippets of information about some of the other patients, most of whom she had known for years.

And then, on his return, Katie got up to go.

*   *   *

On impulse Katie swerved left on her bicycle at the bottom of the hill to take the road into town.

Returning to the empty cottage didn't appeal to her, even though there was nothing she particularly needed to buy. A magazine or two for Jane, perhaps, and another postcard for Anna.

The newsagent's on the corner was the obvious place for both and she spent some time browsing among the postcards choosing one that Anna would like, and not being able to decide between Agapanthus on Tresco or Rhododendrons at Pentle Bay, wherever that was.

She hadn't visited either. Even if she had, she wouldn't have seen those glorious colourful blooms at this time of the year. In the end she bought both and, smiling, emerged into the street again.

Very nearly opposite was the Steamship Office. For moment or two she stared across at it, imagining walking inside and buying her ticket for the flight across to the mainland.

But not yet. Definitely not yet.

She collected her bicycle and covered the short distance to Porthcressa beach. This was the place that seemed to touch her spiritually more than any other. Perhaps it was the salt in the air and the glitter of sunlight on the rocks that helped the tension seep out of her.

She leaned her bike against the sheltering wall, sat down on her favourite seat and closed her eyes. She heard the faint lapping of the sea on the sand and the mewing of the gulls above.

'I thought I'd find you here.'

She looked up at the sound of Rory's voice. She hadn't heard him come and now as she moved along the seat to make room for him, she realised that she had been half-expecting to see him again.

She wanted to ask what the doctor had told him about his grandmother but kept silent. He would tell her in his own good time.

'This is a sad business.'

At once tears sprang to her eyes. She had tried to do her best for Jane who had been kind to her at a vulnerable time and now it had come to this.

'I'm so sorry,' she said, her voice hardly more than a whisper.

'You're fond of her.'

It was a statement rather than a question. She glanced at him and saw that he was staring out to sea and sitting with his hands clasped tightly in his lap.

She longed to place her hands on top of his and assure him that all was well. But it wasn't well and she wondered if it ever would be.

She cleared her throat but the tears

still came. He turned and looked at her. And then his arm was round her and he pulled her close so that resting her face against the coolness of his jacket seemed the most natural thing to do.

And so it was, she thought, as she tried to choke back her tears. So it was.

'You're not still blaming yourself, Katie?' he murmured. 'There is really no need. It would have happened anyway.'

She looked up at him.

'I should have been there.'

He hesitated for just a moment. Then he bent his head and kissed her and for a moment the world seemed a wonderful place of light and warmth when nothing mattered except this glorious peace that engulfed them both. She wiped her eyes.

His face swam into focus and she saw that now his eyes had lost that glazed expression she had found so disturbing.

'You were doing a valuable job for Mark,' he said. 'You can't at the moment know how valuable.'

'I know Jarrel Farm means all the world to Jane.'

'That's so.' He smiled briefly. 'She was born nearby but when she married my grandfather she moved into the house. My father and his elder brother were born there, of course. Mark's father, that is. She has always cared deeply for the family business and the flower farming traditions.'

'We've talked about it. She's so happy when she's reminiscing.'

And she was happy, too, imagining how it had been.

'How long has she been living in Jarrel Cottage?'

'Twenty-five years or more, ever since Mark's father married.'

'A long time.'

He nodded. There was no need to spell it out, she thought. She understood the present situation only too well. She was here on a temporary basis which had seemed so useful at the time to give her four weeks' space to sort out her affairs and plan her future.

But Jane would need constant attention from now on in a place more suitable for her condition than the cottage, with its difficult staircase and small rooms. It was well off the beaten track, too, a huge disadvantage.

Even if she was allowed to return, Jane would need someone who was willing to make the job her career and who had nursing qualifications that Katie lacked.

Rory was looking at her in silence. She could see he wished to say something but was reluctant to do so. But she knew now, with deep certainty, that as well as wishing to remain with Jane the thought of going away from this man who meant all the world to her was something she could not contemplate.

'The doctor has told me that we must think seriously about my grandmother's future,' he said at last, 'and warned me that in his opinion the cottage is no longer an option.'

Katie's throat was dry. She had

known this was coming, of course, and had nothing to say.

'But at least we have a little time to work something out. There are more tests to be done and she needs to stay where she is for a few more days. We don't know what will happen in the immediate future. Jane likes your visits and I don't want to deny her that but in the circumstances you may wish to leave.'

Katie took a deep painful breath, unable to look at him. There was no threat of tears now, only numb shock that he should think that of her. His words sounded as if they were wrung out of him but the meaning was clear.

'I'd like to stay here, to see her every day. But in due course I can see that she will need someone permanent to be with her at all times. Since my contract is coming to an end I would like to be considered for that position.'

Now she had startled him.

'You?'

Katie's face felt warm. This decision had come to her suddenly. At least it seemed like it but maybe her subconscious had been working away on her behalf.

'What about your own life on the mainland, the sale of your father's home, your future career . . . ?'

'This would be my career.'

He made a move to stand and Katie got up, too.

'I'll run you home,' he said. 'We'll pick up my car and put the bike in the back.'

Home, Katie thought. A few more days and it would most likely no longer be that, it seemed. Rory had made that abundantly clear.

'No, I'll . . . '

He caught hold of the bicycle.

'It would be a great favour if you would remain here for the next few days. I'm due in St Austell tomorrow and I can't put it off. I'll be back as soon as I can. Thank you for that, Katie.'

She looked at him then.

His smile didn't quite reach his eyes and he gripped the handlebars as they set off as if afraid of letting them go.

18

Planning Ahead

Empty hours and days seemed to stretch in front of her when Katie got up next morning and ate a solitary breakfast in the kitchen, too dispirited to take it outside to the sunny wall again today. She heard sounds of a car approaching and to her surprise heard Glenda's voice as she opened the front door and called a cheerful greeting.

'Just between jobs,' she said.

'I'm so glad to see you, Glenda, you can't imagine.'

'So how are things now?'

Katie told her as she filled the kettle. 'You've time for a coffee?'

Glenda nodded. She looked serious as she hooked a chair out from under the table and sat down.

'It certainly sounds as if your days here are numbered.'

'Blunt and to the point,' Katie said as she made the coffee and sat down, too.

She could tell that Glenda was full of sympathy for her, as well as for Jane, by the way she had settled down here as if she had all the time in the world when Katie knew for a fact that her time was limited. They had become good friends in the short time she had been on Scilly and Glenda was a good listener.

'I've been thinking,' Katie said. 'This room is big enough to use as a sitting-room as well as a kitchen. Think how Jane would love being able to step straight out into the garden in the summer.'

'I can see that you've been giving this some serious thought,' Glenda said.

'Jane is desperate to stay here. She would hate to leave to leave her old home. I think it would kill her.'

Glenda gave an understanding nod.

'She could talk of nothing else when I popped in on my way here. It's a

215

wonder she hasn't got the days marked off on a calendar. I was non-committal, of course. Others who care for her believe she would be better off being looked after elsewhere.'

'But you don't agree?'

Glenda leaned forward.

'As my grandma used to say, always listen to the elderly. They're often wiser than you think when it comes to their well-being and know what's best for them. She likes you, Katie. She's happy with you here. But you see the difficulties?'

Katie sighed as she picked up her cup, looked at it and put it down again.

'Don't you think the sitting-room would make a good bedroom on the ground floor?' she asked.

'I see what you're getting at but it's a long shot. The bathroom upstairs would be the problem. A chair lift would be out of the question, with that awkward bend in the narrow staircase halfway up.'

'There's a large wall cupboard by the

216

front door,' Katie pointed out. 'I was thinking it wouldn't need much done to be enlarged and a sink, loo and shower installed.'

'Have you mentioned this to Rory and Mark?'

Katie shrugged.

'Not yet.' In any case, she had only just thought about it. 'Rory's gone to the mainland again for a few days and I haven't seen Mark.'

'It will depend on the results of the tests, of course,' Glenda said. 'In any case Jane will need somewhere to go while any work's being done. Mark could be useful there, rattling about in that farmhouse of his.'

She leaned back in her chair and laughed.

'Just listen to the pair of us, arranging Jane's life for her and everyone else's as well.'

'I wish we could,' Katie said, laughing. Glenda's visit was doing her good.

But there was one important thing

and she was almost afraid of mention-
ing it in case Glenda thought it an
impertinent one in the circumstances.

'Something else?' Glenda looked
interested.

'I've suggested to Rory that I take on
the position of looking after Jane
full-time, a permanent paid job. It's
what I'd like to do. I know I'm not a
professional nurse but Jane might not
need full-time nursing.'

'And what was his reaction?'

Katie hesitated, remembering his
silence.

'There wasn't one.'

'I see.' Glenda moved her cup away
from her.

'I want to stay in the islands. I love it
here. I want to make it my home.'

'Not go back to the mainland?'

'Only for holidays.'

'Well, Rory didn't turn you down in
so many words, did he? Don't give up,
Katie. Come on, cheer up. Auntie Glenda
will put in a good word for you.'

Suddenly Katie felt a surge of hope.

★　　★　　★

Katie's hospital visit to Jane that afternoon was frustrating. For one thing, there was no hope of Rory arriving to see his grandmother and bring a flush of pleasure to her pale cheeks. For another, Mark hadn't put in an appearance, which she might have expected.

'I haven't seen Mark for days,' she said.

'Typical Mark,' Jane said with some asperity. 'He'll come when it suits him and not before.'

Jane didn't seem at all upset by this and Katie let the matter drop. There were other visitors, Jane's friends from the old days, and Katie was pleased to see her delighted response to their presence.

Now that she realised that Jane seemed to thrive on company, and aware that Jarrel Cottage was way off the beaten track, she had a moment's doubt about the plans she was proposing.

'Now, Katie,' Jane said as the last of them departed. 'There's something wrong, I can tell. I hope you haven't heard something to my disadvantage?'

Before Katie could reply there was a muted screech in the doorway and Enid appeared, laden down with two large cushions.

'Nearly couldn't get through,' she said as she approached Jane's chair.

She leaned forward to give her a peck on the cheek, almost overbalancing as her cargo got in the way.

Smiling, Katie leaped up to relieve her of it.

The cushions, in a myriad of bright colours, were soft and for a moment she leaned her face against them and smelled the faint lavender that seemed to follow Enid about.

Then she indicated that Enid should take her chair as she was about to go soon anyway.

'Becky will give you a lift home if you want one, Katie,' Enid said as she retrieved one of the cushions and tried to stuff it behind Jane.

Finding there wasn't enough room she dropped it on the floor.

'She'll be here in a minute. She's parking the car.'

'Is this all your own work?' Katie asked in admiration.

'I thought they would make Jane more comfortable.'

'You'll have them back when they let me out of here,' Jane said. 'And that's going to be soon, if I have anything to do with it.

'The handiwork's good, I'll grant you that, Enid. Give me that one, Katie, so that I can make sure. And don't let Enid anywhere near my bad ankle.'

Enid gave a trilling laugh and sat down.

Katie hastened to admire her work but could see Enid wasn't hurt by Jane's reaction in the slightest and seemed instead to find the whole thing hilarious.

She could see that Jane, too, was quietly pleased with her gift but felt no need to say so. They were old friends and knew each other well.

Jane wasn't quite as animated as she had been with her other visitors, but there was a quiet dignity about her now as she listened to Enid's description of her argument with the council about providing her with a permanent outlet in town to display her wares.

'They said it was up to me to find one myself,' she said, her voice rising in indignation.

Jane, smiling, listened in silence.

When Becky appeared, anxious to check on her mother, Enid was quick to arrange a lift for Katie.

Becky smiled.

'Of course.'

Katie glanced back as they left the ward. Jane looked happy and at peace in the company of her oldest friend, pleased to have her to herself. Isolated as it was, Jarrel Cottage was Jane's security, too.

'I wanted to see you on your own, Katie,' Becky said as they drove out of the car park and took the road that led up to Jarrel Cottage past the entrance to Liberty Farm. 'Mark's not answering his house phone and his mobile's switched off. Mainland Marketing have been unable to contact him, either.

'Fortunately we were able to supply them instead. Would you mind telling him when you next see him in case his phone's out of order?'

'Of course. I'll go round there tomorrow if he hasn't surfaced by then. At least Jane's not worried that he hasn't come to see her.'

'Thanks, Katie, Just thought I'd mention it.'

Becky put her foot down and the vehicle surged up the hill.

'You don't mind if I drop you by your track, do you? I have an appointment at the bank or we could check on Mark now.'

Katie felt a stab of guilt in accepting the lift when she could have cycled back, as it wasn't quite dusk.

When Becky pulled up Katie leaped

out, and waved her on her way. It wasn't until she arrived at the cottage that she remembered the bicycle, still in the back of the Liberty Farm truck.

19

A Helping Hand

Next day Katie phoned Mark again but got no reply. The obvious thing to do was to visit the farm and try to catch him in case he had been working outside and hadn't heard the phone.

There was the hint of rain in the air and the faint scent of mud and wet foliage as she set out along the grass path. The ground underfoot was softer today and already the weeds at the side were beginning to grow again.

In the distance there was the sudden roar of a plane taking off and then its steady hum as it set off on its journey to the mainland. Katie watched it until it was out of sight among the clouds and imagined Rory on it being carried away over the sea on his way to St Austell, miles away.

Feeling abandoned because he was no longer here was crazy, but her sense of loss was a dull ache she could do nothing about.

She tried to concentrate on how well Jane had looked when she visited yesterday. She had been sitting upright by her hospital bed and more like her old self. She had emphasised more than once that she wanted to be back home and resting her ankle there, instead of being in hospital cluttering up the place.

'There's nothing wrong with me that a spell in my own home won't put right,' she had told her sharply when Katie smiled.

Now Katie was glad of some action and she set out at a fast pace, avoiding the puddles as the rain increased to a steady drizzle.

She reached the yard and saw that it was empty apart from the usual piles of junk. Mark's car was not in the barn but the truck and trailer were there, so he wasn't out in the fields.

She opened the gate to the tiny front garden and knocked on the front door. Not a sound. She knocked again and then tried the door. It was unlocked.

For a moment she stood, undecided, on the doorstep. The silence seemed oppressive and yet there could be a simple explanation for Mark's absence.

She tried to remember the last time she had seen him. Surely it hadn't been when she was here working in the bulb field on Sunday, helping him fulfil an order for the following day and learning how to bunch the narcissi?

Inside the house she heard the phone ring. She didn't hesitate.

'Mainland Marketing,' she heard when she picked up the receiver.

The order today for Scilly Whites was a small one but they needed to have it by this afternoon. To her dismay she heard herself promising that it would be possible.

She leaned back against the wall by the phone, appalled. Now what had she done?

The sensible thing would be to get someone to accompany her on a tour of the house first, just in case there was an emergency situation. But why should there be? Mark's car wasn't here.

'Don't be a wimp,' she told herself. Mentally throwing back her shoulders, she moved through the house.

Downstairs was easy to check and took only a few minutes. Kitchen, sitting-room, dining-room, shower room . . .

There were a couple of other rooms as well, one of them used as a study. She called Mark's name as she mounted the wide staircase but, as she expected, there was no reply.

She found a bathroom and four large bedrooms, one of them obviously Mark's. The bed had been made but the wardrobe door was hanging open and so was one of the drawers near the window. Both were empty. A quick glance was all that was needed. Mark wasn't at home.

Downstairs again, she glanced at the phone in the hallway. She called Becky at Liberty Farm and left a message to say she would call in for her bicycle on the way down to town this afternoon.

Outside again, Katie walked purposely towards the barn to collect one of the shallow plastic boxes in which to stack the flowers she was going to pick. She knew what she had to do and she would do it.

★   ★   ★

In the few days since she had been here Katie hadn't lost the knack and this time her back didn't ache quite as much. Not yet, anyway. Mark had pointed out the rows that were Scilly Whites when she had been here on Sunday. She made a start on a row that she assumed was correct, picking until she had a large amount to place in the container. Then to work again.

After a while she looked round and, to her surprise, saw two more pickers at the end of the next row. Trespassers helping themselves? She knew she should check but waited until she had picked another bundle before she did so.

'I think you've made a mistake,' she said, breathlessly. 'This is Mark Hobson's field.'

'That's right,' the older man said, straightening. 'No mistake. We're here to help, aren't we, Dan?'

The younger one nodded and grinned.

'But how did you . . . ?'

'Helping out someone who needs it. Mark's one of us, you see. Bob Tait sent us. We're to pick a good number to store in the cool room to see Mark on a bit, wherever he is. Scilly Whites, is it?'

Katie nodded. A lump rose in her throat and she swallowed hard.

'That's good of you. But how did you know that's what these are, when the whole field is in bud?'

The older man grinned.

'Experience, m'dear.'

Katie felt humbled. They must think her a rank amateur and yet they had given no hint of that.

Dan looked at her, an anxious frown making him seem older than she first thought.

'We've got the tractor parked up on the road in case you need the transport.'

She nodded, not trusting herself to speak. Getting her heavy load back to the farm for bunching was a problem that had been solved for her. The generosity was amazing.

She returned to the row she was working on. Soon the container was full and another one, which the men had brought with them, filled too.

'Time to go,' Dan said.

Together they trudged to the parked tractor, each of the men carrying a container. Katie walked behind the vehicle for the short distance to the yard where it stopped and the men jumped down.

'Becky says to tell you sort the stems into two lengths,' Dan said, 'and she'll collect them early afternoon. No need to bunch them this time. They'll see to that.'

Katie nodded and thanked them again. They carried the containers into the barn. She watched them drive off and then started on the sizing.

Scilly was a good place where neighbour helped neighbour. It was a place she wanted to be. And now she had a quick call to make to Anna, to warn her that she wouldn't be free to come to her for Christmas.

*   *   *

She seemed always to be leaving messages on mobiles, Katie thought. She had tried a few times on Rory's and always got the messaging service. She hoped he'd pick up soon and learn that Mark had apparently disappeared to the mainland for whatever reason and there was no news of when he was expected back.

There would obviously be no more orders today, but what of tomorrow?

Maybe the extra Scilly Whites stored in the cool room would suffice, but she would never know unless she was here at Jarrel Farm.

The trouble was she didn't know exactly how the system worked. She could only think of Jane and her dismay should the Hobson name be called into disrepute.

When she had sorted the narcissi as instructed, Katie walked back to the cottage for lunch and to prepare for her visit to the hospital.

★   ★   ★

Jane was sitting on the edge of her chair fully dressed. A pair of crutches were leaning against the bed. Her face lit up when she saw Katie.

'Did you get the message, my dear?' she said. 'I'm all ready to go home!'

'What message?'

Katie felt a moment of surprise and then light dawned. She had been so intent on getting through to Rory on her mobile that she had forgotten to check for messages on the house phone at the cottage.

'But, are you sure?'

'Of course I'm sure,' Jane said tartly.

'There's a crisis on and beds are needed. They made sure I could use the crutches and they know I'm not on my own. I'll manage the stairs at home, just you see.'

She looked so determined that Katie knew it was no use arguing. A nurse came in at that moment and Katie was able to check that all was in order and the test results satisfactory. Even getting into the back seat of the taxi posed little difficulty.

She had been grateful to Becky for picking her up on her way to Jarrel Farm to collect the narcissi. It had meant she was earlier at the hospital than usual but that didn't matter. Neither did leaving her bike in Becky's truck on her suggestion, because Becky would be glad to collect her later if she let her know when she was ready.

But that was a good deed too far, Katie thought, because the Taits were so busy and circumstances had changed. A quick phone call to Becky on their arrival at Jarrel Cottage would sort that out and she hoped Becky would understand.

The only difficulty, it seemed, was breaking the news to Jane that, without telling anyone, her younger grandson had left the islands, leaving no-one running Jarrel Flower Farm in his absence.

20

Calm Reaction

As it turned out, Jane took the news calmly. At first it seemed that she was more concerned with proving that she could manoeuvre herself up the narrow staircase and then down again than she was with the mere question of a grown-up grandson displeasing his relatives.

'Now,' she said when that was accomplished, 'I can give my mind to other things. I can see you're concerned about something, Katie. Mark, of course.'

'He left no message with anyone when he left the island the other day and I can't contact him. And Rory's away.'

'Ah, yes, I'd forgotten that.'

Katie was surprised at her calm reaction.

'The only thing is, I feel I should be

there in the house, fielding calls for orders and doing what picking I can.'

'It's not your responsibility, Katie.'

Katie was silent. Of course it wasn't, but she wished it was, in spite of her initial worry that she might not be able to fulfil expectations. She glanced at the photo albums piled neatly on the table.

Jane caught her glance.

'Of course, you're my family, Katie, as much as anyone.'

Katie was touched.

'Thank you.'

'But you shouldn't have to worry about the farm as well as everything else.'

'And neither should you.'

It might be a good moment to suggest alternative sleeping arrangements, Katie thought. But as soon as she suggested it, Jane was adamant that her bedroom was upstairs and that was that.

Though disappointed, Katie knew when she was beaten.

'This is a cottage with two floors,'

Jane pointed out, 'and I shall treat it as such.'

'But you wouldn't object to sleeping on the ground floor if you were living in a one-storey place?'

Jane looked at her suspiciously.

'You've been talking to Rory.'

Katie flushed.

'No, no, I . . . ' Her lip trembled.

'I'm a foolish old woman,' Jane said, her voice gentle. 'I don't deserve someone as good as you. We'll regard the matter as closed.'

Jane settled herself on the sofa with her foot on a footstool and Katie, looking at her, thought she looked like an indomitable captain on a ship, facing shipwreck but refusing to believe it. She smiled, though her heart felt heavy.

'We shall employ pickers,' Jane said.

Katie frowned.

'Easier said than done, I'm afraid. Becky Tait was saying that it's difficult to do that at the moment. I'd be happy to do the picking myself if I allow myself plenty of time.'

'I'm sure you could, my dear. But would you want to?'

'Oh, yes.'

'Then I shall help you all I can.'

She lifted her injured foot and looked at it critically.

Katie gave a muffled laugh. For a moment Jane looked affronted and then, suddenly, she laughed, too.

'What an old fool I am.'

'Never that — even if you have difficulty hobbling about.'

'Then we'll use Plan B.'

'Which is?'

'I need time to think about that.'

The atmosphere had lightened now and Katie, wondering how she would know what was required if she wasn't near the telephone, thought that it wasn't the moment to go into it.

First she must unpack Jane's belongings for her and then prepare and cook a meal for them both. She mustn't forget that Jane was freshly out of hospital.

Katie was on her way downstairs

again when it occurred to her that Mark had been on his own at the farm and so must have been contacted by mobile phone when he was out in the fields. But if she contacted Mainland Marketing would they change that mobile number to her own, just on her say-so?

She had a vague memory of seeing someone around when she first went to the farm, but perhaps that had been the chap who had gone off to the mainland and there was no-one else.

Someone would know. Bob Tait? After she and Jane had eaten she would contact Liberty Farm again and make enquiries.

★ ★ ★

'Anyone at home?' Glenda's cheerful voice as she pushed open the front door was a welcome sound.

'There are two of us back here now, I'm pleased to say,' Katie greeted her.

'And how is she?'

Katie smiled.

'Blooming. Raring to go. She's in the sitting-room. Please go in.'

Glenda vanished in a swirl of uniform and Katie heard an excited voice and then more muted tones. Leaving them to it, she started to make preparations for Jane's favourite meal of omelette and mashed potato.

She had just finished making a salad when Glenda thrust her head round the kitchen door.

'May I come in?'

She didn't wait for an answer but pulled a chair out from the table and sat down.

'Something smells good.'

'I can soon make some more.'

'No, I must be off but thanks all the same. Visibility's really bad out there and it's thickening up fast over the Eastern Isles. Just as well you got Jane home when you did.'

Katie gazed at the window. What had been a pleasant view of grass and shrubs was now a mass of swirling mist.

'I see what you mean.'

'Jane seems to have perked up a lot. You've a problem on your hands, I hear.'

'She seems to thrive on those.'

'She wouldn't be a Hobson if she didn't.' Glenda ran her fingers along the table top. 'She's talking of getting round to the farm herself.'

Katie laughed.

'On my bike or on foot?'

'She's not going to be beaten, you know.' Glenda smiled.

Katie knew that only too well but Jane on her crutches, getting along the uneven path between the two dwellings, couldn't be considered.

Glenda left soon after that, making a dash for her car and driving off slowly through the mist.

* * *

Next morning Katie pulled open her bedroom curtains and then felt like closing them again.

She had imagined that the mist would have vanished overnight but there were still shreds of it swirling about as if trying to make up its mind what to do.

At breakfast Jane helped herself to another glass of orange juice and looked at Katie over the top of her glasses.

'It will probably clear before long and if it doesn't there's nothing we can do about it, Katie.'

The phone rang, startling Katie as she poured coffee.

She looked in dismay at the stain on the tablecloth as she got up to answer it.

21

A Sense of Belonging

'Don't waste time chatting, Katie,' Enid said as she came into kitchen at Jarrel Cottage next morning. 'I promised to be here extra early to do a spot of babysitting while you get off to the bulb fields, and here I am.'

She placed a large overflowing canvas bag on the kitchen table and started unpacking giant balls of wool, one of which slid off on to the floor.

With an exclamation of dismay, she scrabbled for it and got up again, her face red with the effort.

Katie put her finger to her lips. Jane was still upstairs and she hated to think what her reaction to the babysitting comment would be, joke or not.

'Thanks for coming, Enid,' she said.

'My little car's in working order now.

Nothing like being independent.'

'You drive your own car?'

Enid, ignoring the surprise in Katie's voice, crushed the empty bag flat and looked round for somewhere to put it.

'Becky was saying that it's a shame our holiday cottages aren't ready or Jane could have used one of them for the time being to leave you free and I'd be on the spot to entertain her. All on one floor, you see.'

Katie thought briefly of the unsuitable holiday lets on Jarrel farm and shuddered. Jane would feel like a prisoner in one of those.

But the house itself? Now there was an idea. Being on the spot could never be over-rated.

'You've made me think, Enid.'

'Think about what?' Jane said from the open doorway. 'So you're here, Enid, you and your wool?'

'Jarrel Farmhouse,' Katie said. 'Your old home. How would you feel about coming over with me each day, Jane? If Mark's not back we could use it as a base. It would be an enormous help for us both to be there.'

'And have me walk there and back every time?' Jane placed her crutches against the wall and sat down.

'I'd drive you, of course,' Enid offered.

Jane snorted.

'In that rattletrap? Far more sense for Katie and me to move in over there if that silly boy chooses not to come back.'

Katie was silent with surprise.

'Since when have you had any sense, Jane?' Enid retorted.

'I have now, and plenty of it. Help me pack a few things, Katie, and then get yourself over there. We'll come presently. I can stand one journey in that vehicle of Enid's and then she can get off home.'

'You think I don't want to see a bit of the action?' Enid was firm as she gathered up her wool to repack it. 'You won't get rid of me that easily.'

Katie left them arguing while she

slipped upstairs. She knew what Jane needed for a short stay and it wasn't long before she was down again with her own bag packed with necessities as well.

As well as these, Enid would bring most of the contents of the fridge as well and the bread and potatoes.

Katie was still feeling bemused as she set off along the path to the farm, wetter now than it was last time and muddier, as well, in patches. The mist had vanished and there was hardly a cloud in the sky.

Bob had promised to sort out the messaging problem for her, and even if the house phone at the farm was used as a contact number instead of her mobile, as requested, someone would be on hand to answer it.

As soon as Jane and Enid arrived she would be free to set out for the fields. Until then she would have a closer look at the rooms in the house, especially downstairs.

Katie saw at once that the empty

room on the ground floor would make a fine bedroom for Jane, with the shower room next door if she would agree to it. It must have been used for such a purpose in the past, because there was an iron bedstead leaning against one of the walls.

Someone would help her bring Jane's own mattress over from the cottage. She could phone Handy Taxis for the purpose. No problem, only Jane herself.

By the time she and Enid arrived, Katie had located the central-heating boiler and the switch to turn it on.

Enid, flushed at the excitement of it all, exclaimed at the welcoming warmth and at the kettle all ready for coffee-making.

Jane was more interested in seeing what Mark had done with the sitting-room that had been once her pride and joy when this was her home. There was plenty to occupy them and Katie left them to it.

Her first job outside was to check the cool room in the barn.

She heard the welcome roar of a plane taking off as she carried the containers out into the main area and then into the inner room to place them on the trestle table used for the bunching. She set to work.

The bucket on the table near the door had been empty for days and she took pleasure now in filling it with bunches of narcissi and making sure the money tin was nearby. They were back in business!

She heard another plane take off and she went to the doorway to watch it climb into the sky and head off for the mainland. Making up for time lost yesterday, she thought, when the poor visibility had grounded the flights in and out.

She was turning back to her bunching when she heard the sound of an approaching car. A customer? That was quick. It screeched to a halt and her heart leaped as Rory jumped out and ran to her.

'You're back?' she whispered.

White-faced, he took her in his arms.

'The cottage was empty. I didn't know what to think.'

She felt him tremble and could hardly find the words to reassure him.

'I tried to phone,' she said as he released her. 'I didn't know . . . '

'I spent most of the night at the airport. I was on the first flight out this morning.' His face looked ravaged and he held her hand in a grip as if he would never let it go. 'I picked up a signal again as soon as we landed. I came straight to the cottage when I got no reply and found it empty. I've been praying hard all the way over here.'

He gazed at the boxes of bunched narcissi on the table.

'You've done all this?'

'I needed to. We might get a call for them. I'm going to do some picking now.'

'Then I'll come with you.'

'Your grandmother?'

'She's on her own?' There was no hint of reproach or concern now.

250

'Enid is with her in the house.'

'Here?'

'It seemed best to move in, to keep things going over here.'

Rory took a deep breath.

'Let's go.'

They set off by foot. The nearest field where Katie had been working was close by. When they arrived they found that the two pickers from yesterday had already filled two pallets. They were in the trailer ready to be brought to the farm. Dan was starting up the tractor and spotted them.

'We'll leave them in the barn, then we'll be off. OK?'

They left in a rush of tractor noise and Rory closed the gate behind them. He and Katie leaned on it, looking at the depleted rows of narcissi with the rest waiting to be picked and sent off to market. Birds twittered in the pittosporum and in the sky above gulls wheeled and cried.

'The Taits have been so helpful,' she said.

'You, too, Katie, it seems.'

'It feels as if I'm family,' she said.

'It's now clear that Mark's not coming back. A single ticket to the mainland was a strong clue. Further enquiries on my part proved that. I discovered that he intends to marry and settle down on the girl's father's farm in North Yorkshire. I have some serious thinking to do.'

Katie took a breath.

'There's something I'd like to tell you.'

She didn't know how the Duchy worked in the matter of leases of farms handed down from father to son. It could be that a member of the same family, however distant, could be viewed favourably to take it on temporarily. But in her case there was no proof.

'My mother's maiden name was Hobson. I have reason to believe there could be a connection, but I can't prove it.'

'What makes you think it?'

She hesitated again before explaining, feeling an old sampler found in a drawer when her father died, with a name on it, sounded improbable as proof of anything.

'Hannah Amy Hobson,' she finished. 'I thought it sounded likely.'

'When you heard my grandmother's name at our first meeting?'

She nodded. His understanding was unexpected and when she saw the curve to his mouth and the brightness of his eyes she smiled, too.

'Yes, I know it was Jane's married name that was Hobson. But I didn't realise that at first.'

'As you know, she moved out of the farmhouse when my grandfather died and into the cottage when my uncle and aunt took over, Mark's parents.'

Katie nodded.

'Because she knew it was the right thing to do.'

'Yet moving out of it now permanently, when it's obviously not suitable for an old lady in her position, is not right?'

'Not in her eyes. Not unless there's a far better reason for it. D'you think they would — I mean, is there any hope that the Duchy would be happy with me as a tenant, for a short time at least? Jane was happy to come with me for a few days. She might agree to stay longer.'

He was silent for a long moment. She thought of Mark, over on the mainland planning to marry in the near future and make his home far away in the north. And of Rory, doing his best to work out the best thing for all concerned when he was deeply involved in his own career.

He turned towards her.

'It will take months to sort out.'

'Yes, I know that.'

'Hello, you two!'

They turned, to see Enid.

'A lovely couple,' she said, her face glowing. 'Am I the first to know?'

Registering their silence, her face fell.

'I've said the wrong thing, haven't I?' She turned and fled.

'Perhaps the right thing,' Rory said, a smile in his voice. 'Let's walk, Katie.'

He took her by the hand as they passed the farmhouse and continued down the lane, to where a wooded path joined it at the bottom. A stream trickled alongside and there was the scent of lush vegetation. She hardly knew where it led, but she might have known it was the way down to another tiny hidden beach, where gentle sea water lapped its pebbly edge.

They stood looking down over it. Rory's voice, when he spoke, sounded more relaxed now.

'I used to come here a lot as a boy. I'd like to think that my children would play here too and their children after them. A Hobson dynasty stretching into the future.'

Katie sighed but smiled, too. Such an ambition and one to be admired. Reality, though, had a way of foiling such dreams. Maybe Mark had had such dreams once, who knew?

Rory bent to pick one of the red campion flowers in the long grass.

'I'd like to think of Gram back at the farmhouse. I've wondered how it would work to knock a way through from the holiday lets into the passage in the house where there's room for an extra door.'

Katie smiled.

'That's the architect in you talking. But neither of those buildings is suitable for someone like Jane.'

'I know that. But what's to stop someone combining the two, knocking down a few walls and making other adjustments? It could be done. It would make a fine home for Gram, all on the ground floor and with easy access to the house.'

'And the cottage?'

'Now, there's a thought. And the adjoining barn, too. I've a feeling Enid's had her eye on that for a while, thinking it would make a fine outlet for local crafts. She hasn't dared say anything about it yet but I can see it coming. It's a wonder Gram hasn't twigged.'

Katie considered.

'I wonder. She was quick to suggest moving temporarily over here once she knew that Mark was leaving. And, strangely, that didn't seem to upset her as I thought it would. It was as if she thought it was all for the best.'

Rory's smile lit up his features.

'A remarkable woman, my grandmother. She might even now be discussing with that good friend of hers exactly how it can be done. As long as they have Jarrel Cottage in the equation as an excellent holiday let during the season, as well as my cottage down in Porthcressa, all will be well financially.'

'Enid's a good friend to us, too.'

'Would you be happy to move into the farmhouse, Katie, so there's someone in residence? Hopefully things will calm down and once everything is set in motion for another branch of the Hobson family to take over the lease of the land.'

'But I'm a Robertson, not a Hobson.'

'You're you, Katie, and that's all important to me.'

'But not to the Duchy.'

'We can soon alter that.'

For a moment Rory looked vulnerable as he cupped her face in his hands.

'I love you, Katie, with all my heart. Please, will you marry me?'

A moment of incredulous silence and then she was in his arms, held close to the man who was all the world to her. He bent and kissed her.

He let her go at last, reluctantly, and she noticed the sunbeams dancing on the lichened-covered rocks on the far side of the beach. They lay beneath the branches of the giant pittosporum, the shrub that seemed to her to be native to the islands in a way she had wished to be.